Ghost of Perdition

Demon Slayer Rome Volume 2

George Alexandros

Toronto, Ontario

First edition – 2026

A special thank you to my editor, Lisa Hannan Fox, and my cover designer, Damonza.

Contents

ACT ONE

I

262 AD

For many of the people gathered around Iader's agora, this was the first time they would hear the Gospel of Jesus Christ. The marketplace, bustling with the noise of merchants hawking their wares and citizens going about their business, was not an ideal setting for preaching. Yet, the devoted priests, Pamphilus and Efrem, stood unwavering amid the chaos as they shared the message of repentance and the immeasurable grace of God through His only unique Son.

Pamphilus and Efrem had journeyed across the Roman Empire, preaching the Gospel to all who would listen. Their mission had not been without hardship. They had suffered persecution in the name of Christ, for Rome had deemed His followers a threat to its dominion over the nations. They had been driven from villages and cities, imprisoned, flogged, and even threatened with crucifixion. And yet, they bore it all with joy, believing that to suffer for the Kingdom of Heaven was a great honor.

But here, in the city of Iader, the priests faced not hostility or acceptance, but a wall of indifference. The bustling streets carried on as though the Gospel they proclaimed was nothing more than a passing breeze. Many hearts seemed resistant, and the priests' words fell like seeds on barren soil.

All but for one boy.

He couldn't have been more than seven or eight years old, with dark, curious eyes and a mop of unkempt hair. Every morning, he appeared at the *agora*, listening intently as Pamphilus and Efrem shared their stories of Jesus. The boy's name, they had learned, was Decimus. He came to them with bread and water, a simple offering that spoke volumes of his budding faith.

His questions were endless, his curiosity boundless. "Did He really heal the blind?" Decimus had asked one morning, his voice filled with wonder. "And raise people from the dead?"

Pamphilus smiled. "Yes, child. He brought sight to the blind, raised the dead, and gave hope to the hopeless. And He can do the same for you."

The priests saw the light of faith in Decimus's eyes, a spark that gave them hope even in the face of widespread apathy. They prayed earnestly that the boy would carry that light within him always.

For today was their last day in the city of Iader.

"Are you leaving?" Decimus asked after Pamphilus and Efrem finished their final sermon.

"Indeed, we are, young Decimus," Pamphilus said. "Our work here is done."

"But can't you stay?" the boy pleaded. "Surely, there are more stories to tell."

"There are many more," Efrem replied. "But there are others who have not yet heard the Gospel. It is our mission, as followers of Jesus, to share the Good News in every corner of the Empire."

They persisted regardless of the threats from Rome and its leaders. Even now, Roman soldiers patrolled nearby, their demon dogs padding along. The chains around the dogs' necks rattled with each step.

Pamphilus and Efrem's departure could not be delayed much longer. To the Roman Empire, their message was treason. Only the gospel of Emperor Diocletian was permitted, and the priests knew it was only a matter of time before the soldiers acted against them.

As they packed what few belongings they carried, Efrem caught Decimus's expression. The boy's brow furrowed in deep thought, and he chewed on his lower lip.

"Is something troubling you, Decimus?" Pamphilus asked.

Decimus hesitated, glancing around as if to ensure no one else was listening. Finally, he spoke in a hushed tone. "I had a dream. I believe... I believe it was of the Theotokos."

The priests exchanged a brief look, their shared years of ministry allowing them to communicate much without words. The Theotokos—Mary, the Mother of God—was indeed revered in Christianity. Reports of her appearing in dreams were rare but not unheard of, and such dreams often carried profound meaning. However, the priests were also cautious, knowing that demons could manipulate dreams to deceive and mislead.

"Can you describe this dream to us?" Pamphilus inquired further.

Decimus's brow furrowed in concentration as he recounted his vision. "I was in a dark room. Or...perhaps it was a cave. All I know is that it was dark—so dark I couldn't see anything at first. Then she appeared before me. She wore a red gown and a red shawl draped over her head and shoulders. She was beautiful. Radiant."

"Did she say anything to you?" Efrem asked.

Decimus nodded solemnly. "She told me to leave everything behind and follow her."

The priests shared another glance—this time with subtle amusement. While the Theotokos held an honored place within the faith as the mother of Christ and the one who had borne God incarnate, she was not the central figure of worship. The instruction to "follow her" was out of character for the teachings of Christianity. Prayers to the Theotokos were petitions for intercession, glorifying her role in salvation history, but they always pointed back to Jesus Christ, the center of the faith.

A dream and nothing more. Not a vision. Not a prophecy. Just a wistful dream of a boy trying to piece together the religion of the Ancient of Days.

"And then today," Decimus said, "you told us that the god-man Jesus said to His disciples to leave all they had and to follow Him. To hate even their mother and father."

Pamphilus nodded. "That's true, but what He meant was that we should love Him first above even our mother and father. Above all else in this world, even our very lives. Christ asks us to make Him the center of our hearts."

"I want to love Him." The boy hesitated, then corrected himself. "No—I *need* to love Him."

Efrem smiled. It was moments like these, seeing a young soul awakened to faith, that brought the greatest joy to his heart. "You can, Decimus. Of course, you can."

Decimus shook his head vehemently. "You don't understand. I want to come with you. I want to learn more about Jesus. I want to leave my whole life here in Iader for Him."

The boy's enthusiasm was admirable, but Pamphilus and Efrem lived a life of constant struggle and sacrifice. It was no path for one so young. And yet, in the weeks they had spent in Iader, Decimus had shown a fervor and dedication rare for a boy his age.

"Please!" Decimus begged. "I promise I will be a faithful servant of Christ!"

"That we do not doubt," Efrem said.

"Then please let me go with you!"

"And what of your parents, Decimus? What will they say?"

The question gave the boy pause. His throat bobbed as he swallowed hard, and he forced a smile. "I love my parents, I do. But..." He hesitated, lowering his head before finding the courage to continue. "But I don't know if they feel the same for me."

Neglect—or perhaps even abuse. It became painfully clear now. The boy's frame was thinner than it should have been, his arms and legs marked with dark bruises that were not simply the stains of a hard life in the city. There was no telling the extent of what Decimus had endured, but the strength he displayed in the face of it was a testament to his willpower and spirit.

Efrem nodded to Pamphilus, who knelt down to meet Decimus at eye level. Tears glistened in the boy's eyes.

"The journey will be a difficult one," Pamphilus said, his hand resting on Decimus's small shoulder. "Are you willing to give everything you have to those in need? Are you prepared to carry your own cross?"

Decimus met the priest's gaze with unwavering determination. "I am."

Pamphilus smiled and gave his shoulder a reassuring squeeze. "Then come, Decimus. Help us pack what little we have. The road ahead is long, and you have much to learn."

II

303 AD

How long had Valen been riding? Hours? Days? Time had blurred into a haze of exhaustion and pain. He had slipped in and out of consciousness more times than he could count, jolted awake by the bumps and lurches as his horse trotted wearily along the uneven road.

He couldn't afford to stop. Stopping meant death. The Roman soldiers were likely still on his trail, and if they caught him, he knew exactly what awaited: a scourging that would strip the flesh from his back, followed by the cold steel of a blade severing his neck. Such was the punishment for deserters.

Not that survival seemed a likely prospect anyway. The wound in his shoulder throbbed with every beat of his heart. Blood had long since soaked through the strip of cloth he had hastily torn from his cloak and wrapped around the wound. He hadn't eaten anything since the ill-fated battle at the Danube River, and the last few drops of water in his wineskin had been drained hours ago.

He was weak. Wounded. And utterly tired.

The horse beneath him—one he'd taken from a fallen Goth—was in no better condition. Its labored breathing grew heavier with each step, its gait uneven. The animal gave a pitiful whinny, stumbled, and finally buckled beneath him.

Valen was thrown forward, slamming hard onto the ground. The impact knocked the wind from his lungs, leaving him gasping as the world spun around him. Grit and grass clung to his cheek, but he barely registered them. He craned his neck to see the horse, collapsed and trembling, its sides heaving as its strength gave out.

"Damn," he croaked, his voice little more than a rasp. With great effort, he dragged himself free of the animal's lifeless body and rolled onto his back.

The sun hung high in the sky, blazing fiercely. Its heat pressed down on him. For a fleeting moment, it felt almost comforting, as if the warmth were lulling him into a final, eternal rest.

His eyelids fluttered, heavy with fatigue. Just a moment of rest. A brief reprieve from the pain. Surely, that couldn't hurt...

He closed his eyes, and the world around him faded into nothingness.

He awoke to the sensation of cool liquid trickling over his lips and pooling in his mouth. Water. Without thinking, Valen swallowed greedily, the soothing liquid sliding down his parched throat.

"Drink slowly," a man's voice instructed. The waterskin was pulled away before he could take another gulp. "You'll make yourself sick if you drink too much at once."

Valen's breath came in shallow gasps. He tried to sit up but lacked the strength. Beside him was the lifeless body of his stolen horse. Flies buzzed around the poor beast.

The man who had given him water wasn't a Roman soldier; that much was clear. He wore a plain, slightly tattered tunic and had an expression of both concern and relief. A faint smile tugged at his lips.

"You are lucky to be alive," he said. "Praise God." The man frowned as he looked over Valen. "Far too young to be a soldier. What is Rome thinking, sending boys to fight its battles?"

Rome hadn't forced him into the legions. That choice—or rather, that command—had come from his father, a hardened centurion who viewed war as a rite of passage. Valen's mother had begged for him to be spared, but her protests had fallen on deaf ears.

Valen wasn't fit for war. His mother had known that. She'd known he would die on the battlefield. And now, desertion had sealed his fate. He would never be able to return to her. His father would disown him, brand him a coward, and he would be forever cast out from the only home he'd ever known.

"Who...?" Valen croaked.

The man placed a gentle hand on Valen's chest. "My name is Decimus," he said. "I am a priest. A man of God. I am going to save you."

A priest? A Christian?

Valen's thoughts swirled, fragmented and faint, as a heavy darkness began to envelop him. He barely noticed Decimus's presence, his words echoing dimly in his mind as unconsciousness dragged him down once more.

***

"I don't think this is a good idea, Cassia."

"Scared, Marcia?" Cassia said with a mischievous grin. Her friend's timidity was amusing, if not a little frustrating.

The two young girls stood amidst the shadows of the hidden cellar beneath the temple—now a church—where Cassia's father, Decimus, held his sermons. The air was damp and cool, carrying the faint scent of mildew and old stone. Cassia doubted her father even knew about this cellar. The concealed entrance had been hidden beneath a loose flagstone, uncovered by sheer luck as Cassia explored.

Marcia hugged herself, eyes darting around the room. "This temple belongs to the Lord."

"It didn't always. Look."

She pointed toward an altar situated at the far end of the cellar. It was ancient, coated in cobwebs and cracks, its once-smooth stone now jagged and worn. Dark reddish-brown stains marred its surface—stains that looked unnervingly like old blood.

The color drained from Marcia's face. She took a step back, shaking her head. "Cassia, this is—this is wrong. We shouldn't be here."

"You're such a child," Cassia said with a scoff. She brushed her fingers across the cold stone of the altar, her mind swirling with a strange mix of fascination and emptiness. She had long since stopped caring about the things her father preached about—God, Jesus, and all the rest. The faith that had once filled her felt hollow now, replaced by a gnawing void she couldn't explain.

"If your father finds us—" Marcia began, but her words were cut short by the sudden crash of the entry gate above. The sound of a struggle followed, heavy and chaotic.

"Oh, no..." Marcia whispered, her voice trembling.

Cassia frowned as she turned toward the stone steps leading back up to the temple. Marcia was already darting up the steps, her frantic footsteps echoing in the confined space.

Cassia lingered for a moment, hesitant. Why the loud entrance? Had her father returned from the village, and if so, what had happened? She didn't want him to find her down here. He'd lecture her about sacred spaces and obedience for hours. With a sigh, she turned to follow Marcia upstairs.

But just as her foot touched the first step, a voice—silken and honeyed—whispered from the shadows behind her.

"Cassia, bleed for me..."

She turned back to the altar. The dried blood stains seemed to glow faintly.

Cassia blinked. When she looked again, the glow was gone. The cellar was dark and lifeless, just as it had been moments before.

Cassia headed up the stairs and carefully moved the flagstone back into place. She dusted her hands off and tried to shake the strange whisper from her mind.

"Cassia!" her father's voice called out.

She was in the antechamber of the temple. The room smelled of paint and parchment, the air thick with the scent of the oils her father used to create his unfinished icons. Scrolls and brushes were scattered on the table where he often worked late into the night.

But there was no time to linger. Cassia made her way to the main hall where her father had called.

Her father was kneeling on the floor beside a young man who lay bleeding. The man's breath was shallow, his skin pale.

"Quick, Marcia!" her father barked. "Get some water and some towels!"

"Yes, Father!" Marcia squeaked and obediently did as she was told.

Cassia stepped closer, her sandals scratching softly against the stone floor. "Who is he?"

"I don't know. I found him passed out near the temple."

"Is he a Roman soldier?" she asked, noting the breastplate and red cape—the unmistakable uniform of the legions of Rome.

Her father frowned. "If he is, he's far too young for war."

Cassia crouched down. Now that she was near the soldier, she saw the boyish features of his face. He couldn't be older than her—perhaps even younger.

The wound on his shoulder was deep, and blood continued to flow freely from it, dripping onto the stone floor in a rhythmic, mesmerizing pattern.

Drip. Drip. Drip.

She stared at the crimson pool, unable to tear her eyes away. A strange hunger clawed at her insides, a deep, gnawing ache that she had never felt before. Her lips parted, her breath catching in her throat.

Hunger.

The realization hit her like a jolt of lightning. She hungered for the sight, the smell, the very essence of the blood pooling before her.

III

His name was Valen.

Decimus had tended to his wound and fever, and now the young man rested in her father's bed in the modest home they shared in the village. Cassia couldn't seem to stay away from him, though she couldn't fully understand why. Yes, Valen was handsome, but it wasn't his face that captivated her. It was the wound on his shoulder, the gash that had nearly claimed his life.

She couldn't explain her fascination. There was something darkly alluring about it. The way life teetered so delicately between survival and death seemed more compelling than anything her father preached about eternal life.

Cassia's mother had died when she was very young, not nearly two summers old. Her father, Decimus, had done his best to fill that void, though his obsession with life—specifically the promise of eternal life offered by Christ—had become all-consuming. Cassia had once shared in his zeal, kneeling beside him in prayer and delighting in the tales of God's chosen people, Israel.

But all of that changed the day her father took the abandoned temple near the village and declared it his church. After that, her prayers shifted, her faith twisted. She no longer sought life; she sought something darker. It wasn't the resurrection of the body or the promise of Paradise that captured her imagination. It was death and blood. Even when her father offered the blood of Christ in the form of watered wine, it stirred something within her that felt more like hunger than reverence.

Once, her father had been a traveling preacher, following in the footsteps of two priests who, he claimed, had saved his life and brought him to Christianity. But those days of wandering were behind him. He had settled in Iader, the city of his birth, and started a family. For a time, he had seemed content. But after her mother's death, Decimus had taken Cassia and left the city, moving to a remote village far to the north.

It was there that he began preaching again, ministering to the villagers and building his congregation. It was through one of the villagers that he had learned of the abandoned temple, a crumbling relic of an age no one in the village could remember.

Which god or goddess had once been worshiped there remained a mystery. Even the elders of the village were uncertain. The temple had been abandoned long before their time, and its secrets were buried beneath layers of dust and shadow.

But Cassia couldn't shake the feeling that the temple's former deity—or something darker still—had never truly left.

***

The village was small, nestled among rolling hills and quiet forests, its peaceful air broken only by the occasional bleating of goats or the laughter of children. This tranquility was precisely why Decimus had chosen to establish his church here rather than in Iader. That, and the memories Iader carried.

Iader had been his birthplace, but it had never been home. His parents had been neither married nor in love; theirs was a fleeting and reckless passion, and

Decimus had been an unwanted consequence. He grew up knowing he was a burden, unloved by both his mother and father. It was a wound that never fully healed, though his years of pilgrimage with Pamphilus and Efrem had brought him some measure of peace.

After Efrem's passing and Pamphilus's decision to retire to Mount Athos, Decimus returned to Iader, where he had every intention of starting his own church. But instead, he found something unexpected—love. He married a woman whose kindness and faith reminded him of the grace he had long sought in others. Their union was brief but joyful, and she gave him a daughter, Cassia. Yet that joy was short-lived; complications during Cassia's birth claimed his wife's life, leaving Decimus a widower and a single father.

Years later, when Cassia was older, Decimus decided it was time to leave Iader behind. The city, with all its bittersweet memories, was no place to raise his daughter or to rekindle the mission of his faith. They journeyed for two days to this small village, a remote and unassuming place where Decimus hoped they could start anew. Here, the ghosts of his parents' neglect and his wife's death could not haunt him as they had in the streets of Iader. Perhaps, in time, he might return to preach the Gospel there, as his mentors had done. But for now, his focus was on this village and its people, building a faithful flock and creating a sanctuary for himself and his daughter.

Decimus walked through the village now, Cassia at his right and Marcia, the first of his converts, at his left. Marcia was slightly older than Cassia, and the two had become friends.

The villagers had welcomed Decimus and Cassia when they first arrived, intrigued by the preacher and his daughter. Though few had fully embraced his teachings, Decimus believed his unwavering kindness and willingness to serve would eventually turn their hearts toward the Lord. He had become both a shepherd and a healer to them, tending to their illnesses, easing their hardships, and sharing the Gospel whenever and wherever they would listen.

"Father, we look forward to taking the holy sacrament of marriage," said Agrippa.

Decimus halted, turning to greet him and his soon-to-be bride, Dosia. They were a lovely couple, both new to the faith but brimming with eagerness to learn and worship. Agrippa stood tall and solid, his calloused hands a testament to his life as a farmer. Dosia, by contrast, radiated a quiet grace, her warm smile and sparkling eyes reflecting her happiness. She clung to Agrippa's arm, leaning against him as if he were her anchor.

"It will indeed be a joyous occasion," Decimus said, smiling. Agrippa took Decimus's hand and kissing it in reverence. "But remember," Decimus continued, "marriage is not easy." He turned to Dosia. "Are you prepared to obey your husband, as the Holy Scriptures command?"

Dosia's cheeks flushed slightly. She hugged Agrippa's arm tighter. "I am, Father."

"And you, Agrippa," Decimus said, fixing the young man with a steady gaze, "will you love your wife as Christ loves the Church?"

Agrippa's chest swelled. "Of course, Father."

Decimus nodded approvingly. "It is not a light commitment. To love your wife as Christ loves the Church means to sacrifice everything for her, to love her unconditionally and without fail. It is a calling few men truly understand, but one that reflects the very heart of our faith."

The couple bowed their heads and kissed Decimus's hand in gratitude. As they walked away, Decimus watched them, his thoughts drifting to his own late wife. Marriage was, indeed, one of the most beautiful sacraments of the Lord.

Turning to his daughter, he said with a teasing smile, "You, too, should start thinking about marriage, Cassia."

Cassia blinked, visibly recoiling. "Me? Marriage?"

"Why not?" Decimus replied, shrugging. "One day, you must leave me and cling to your husband."

"Cling to a farmer?" Cassia wrinkled her nose in distaste. "I think not, Papa."

Before Decimus could respond, his attention was drawn to a thin, hunched figure hovering near the wall of a nearby house. The young man was practically glued to the shadows, his gaze shifting nervously from side to side.

"Fabian," Decimus murmured. Fabian was the most recent member of his church, a painfully shy young man who had come to the Lord with the wide-eyed wonder of a child. Despite his timid nature, Fabian's faith was pure and untainted.

"Come, Fabian," Decimus said, gesturing for the young man to join them.

"I apologize, Father," Fabian said, wincing as though speaking aloud caused him pain.

"For what, dear one?" Decimus asked. He placed a reassuring hand on Fabian's trembling shoulder. "Blessed are you, Fabian. Remember that."

Cassia rolled her eyes. The gesture, subtle though it was, did not escape Decimus's notice. He sighed inwardly.

Before he could address her attitude, a booming voice echoed through the village, sharp and commanding.

"Repent! For the night of the blood is upon us!"

The cry came from the central agora. Together with Fabian, Marcia, and a reluctant Cassia, he made his way to the source of the commotion. There, a crowd had gathered in uneasy curiosity around a group of men Decimus had never seen before.

The men were brutish, their expressions hard, their bodies marked by scars and muscle. One stood apart, shorter than the rest, yet his presence was commanding. He wore a black robe that swayed with his fervent gestures. In his hand, he held a staff adorned with strange carvings and what looked like dried blood smeared across its surface.

"Who are they, Father?" Marcia asked, concerned.

"I know not," Decimus said.

The man in the black robe stepped forward, raising his staff high into the air. "Once, this village belonged to the followers of blood before Rome came and conquered it!" his voice thundered. "And it will soon return to the blood queen!"

"The blood queen?" a villager called out. "Who is that?"

A wave of puzzled murmurs spread through the crowd. None of the villagers seemed to know this supposed blood queen, nor did Decimus. Troubled, his brow furrowed.

The crowd began to disperse, their initial curiosity giving way to skepticism. Most seemed to dismiss the robed man's words as the rantings of a lunatic.

Decimus, however, stepped forward. "Friend," he said, "I'm afraid you must be mistaken. There is no queen of blood in these parts."

The man's gaze snapped toward Decimus, his dark eyes narrowing. "She will rise again! Mark my words!"

"What will she do when she returns?" Cassia asked with a hint of interest.

The man's attention shifted to her, his gaze lingering. Decimus moved closer to his daughter. Though the man himself was not particularly imposing, his followers were a different matter. Their rugged appearances and the cold calculation in their eyes suggested they were no strangers to violence.

"No more sickness," the man said, "and no more death."

Decimus smiled, intending to project a sense of peace and humility. "Now I know you are mistaken, friend, for only Jesus Christ, our Lord and Savior, has defeated death and can truly cure the sick."

The man spat at Decimus's feet. "A Christian, are you?"

"I am," Decimus replied evenly. "And this is my family." He gestured to those with him, including both his blood daughter and his spiritual family, for in Christ, all were brothers and sisters.

The man scrutinized each of them, one by one. His eyes stayed on Cassia. She met his stare.

"You will all bow down to the blood queen," the man said at last. "I promise you that. My people have waited many years for this day to come."

Decimus's face hardened. "Perhaps it is you who should bow to the living God and His Son. Perhaps it is you who must repent."

The man chuckled darkly, shaking his head. "Christians. Always so high and mighty."

Without another word, he turned and walked away, his companions following close behind.

Marcia asked, "What should we do, Father?"

"Distance yourselves from them," Decimus instructed. "I have encountered men like them before in my travels. Dangerous and impulsive."

"I'm worried," Fabian said.

"Fabian, put your faith in the Lord. He is our refuge and strength."

Decimus ushered them away from the agora. But Cassia did not follow. She stood rooted in place, her eyes locked on the departing figures of the blood queen's followers.

"Cassia?" Decimus called to her.

She didn't respond, as though she hadn't heard him at all. Her gaze remained fixed on the men retreating into the distance.

***

"Father, please forgive me," Marcia said, "but I must tell you something that is weighing heavily on my heart."

"Of course, Marcia. What is it? You can tell me anything."

The evening air was still as the two worked within the temple, arranging crosses and placing icons along the walls. The flickering light of oil lamps cast long shadows, giving the temple a somber ambiance. Despite their efforts to transform it into a place of Christian worship, the lingering essence of its pagan origins still hung in the air.

Following the events of the day, Marcia had convinced herself that the god this temple had once been devoted to could have been the blood queen the strangers had spoken of. Her unease deepened when she recalled the altar hidden in the basement.

When Marcia had shown Decimus the altar earlier, he'd dismissed it as a relic of the temple's pagan past. Sacrifices of goats, lambs, or chickens were common in such places.

But what about human sacrifice?

"It's Cassia, Father," she said. "She... I'm afraid she has strayed from the Lord, and I'm scared for her."

Decimus paused, turning his full attention to Marcia. "You are her closest friend. Has something happened?"

"Not precisely," Marcia said. "But I have noticed she does not pray as much as she once did. As much as we do."

Decimus nodded. “Prayer is important, indeed. But that is hardly a reason to be afraid for her.”

“I know that,” Marcia said, her words rushing out, “but it’s more than that...”

Her voice faltered, and she averted her gaze.

“You can tell me, Marcia.”

His calmness gave her the courage to continue. “She’s been talking about death,” Marcia said. “And about blood. And when those men came today... I’m afraid they will take her away from us.”

Decimus offered her a comforting smile, the same smile that had so often eased her worries before. “Worry not, my dear Marcia. Your heart is in the right place. I am not surprised that Cassia has strayed. We are all fallen creatures, all of us sick with sin, for sin itself is a sickness. At times, that sickness diminishes our faith. But I trust in the Lord that Cassia will return to Jesus, and when she does, He will heal her sickness, making her and her faith that much stronger.”

“And what of her fascination with death and blood?”

“She lost her mother when she was very young. Such a loss can leave wounds that take years to heal. A loss of that magnitude, especially for a young girl, can manifest in ways we don’t fully understand. That, too, will pass.”

"What can we do, Father?"

"Pray, Marcia. Pray for her. Prayer is our greatest weapon against the forces that seek to pull us away from the Lord."

IV

When Valen regained his strength, he devoted himself to assisting Decimus with transforming the temple into the church Cassia's father had envisioned. Valen quickly became a follower of Christ, embracing his new faith with the fervor of someone desperate for redemption. He was a good and faithful servant, diligent in his work, and gifted with his hands—a quality Cassia found herself thinking about far too often.

Those hands. She yearned to feel them on her.

Once a Roman soldier, Valen had fled his legion in the chaos of a losing battle against the northern tribes. His father had forced him into the military, but Valen's heart had always belonged to carpentry. The craft was his passion, and Decimus had seen divine purpose in this. After all, wasn't Jesus Himself believed to have been a carpenter?

"Valen, you remind me of the Lord," Decimus had said once, watching Valen skillfully carve a wooden cross for the church. Valen had smiled at the compliment.

He helped Decimus with his icons and crosses. By day, he was a dedicated laborer in the service of the church. By night, however, he became something else entirely—a source of longing, confusion, and hunger for Cassia.

They often sat together in the evenings, watching the sun sink below the horizon, its fiery colors reflected in the distant hills.

"I am grateful to you and your father," Valen said one evening. "Decimus gave me a new life."

"Do you like it here?" Cassia asked. "Will you stay?"

Her pulse quickened as a voice in her mind whispered, *Make him stay.*

Valen nodded. "I think I will."

"Good. I want you to stay."

"Cassia?"

Something primal stirred within her. Desire, longing, maybe even lust. She knew these were vices to be avoided, but in that moment, she didn't care. The voice in her mind grew louder, urging her on.

Feel his blood pounding.

Cassia reached out and her fingers brushed against his. She took his hand in hers, staring into his eyes. "I see the way you look at me."

Valen's cheeks flushed as he looked away from her, but he did not pull away. Instead, he gave her hand a gentle squeeze. "You are a beautiful girl."

"Then look at me," she demanded, her voice trembling with an intensity that surprised even her.

Take him.

He obeyed, lifting his eyes to hers. For a fleeting moment, fear flashed across his face, but it passed quickly. His expression softened, and he reached out to caress her cheek. His touch sent a shiver down her spine.

Take him, child. He's yours. All yours. Blood and soul.

She leaned in and kissed him, her lips brushing against his tentatively at first, then with more fervor. He responded in kind, wrapping his strong arms around her. His hands moved along her back, pulling her closer, their embrace deepening as the heat between them grew.

"Ack!" Valen yelped, pulling away.

His lip bled where she had bitten him. She tasted the metallic sweetness of his blood on her tongue.

And it tasted good. Too good.

***

Every day, their passion consumed them a little more. They surrendered to it. There was no turning back now, no thought of repentance. Before long, Valen had come to know Cassia in the most intimate of ways.

"If your father were to find out..." Valen said, his voice tinged with both fear and excitement as he lay beside her, his fingers idly tracing patterns on her arm.

"Let him find us. You are my prince, and I am your queen."

They hid in the village stables, the scent of hay and the soft nickering of horses their only witnesses. It had become a place where their love—and their sin—flourished beyond the prying eyes of the village.

"I love you," Valen said.

"Do you? Do you truly?"

"I do."

"How far would you go for me?"

"To the depths of Hades itself," Valen declared. Then, almost as an afterthought, he added, "God, forgive me."

"God has nothing to do with this," Cassia whispered, taking his hand in hers. "Here, when you are with me, I am your god."

Utter blasphemy. Only the demons of Rome, or the Emperor himself, dared to make such claims of divinity. For Cassia, a mere village girl and the daughter of a priest, to declare herself a god was nothing short of apostasy. It was an affront to the Lord, the God of Abraham, Isaac, and Jacob.

Yet Valen did not recoil. Instead, he stared at her with a desperate intensity. "Yes," he said. "Of course. Yes, you are."

"Kiss me."

And he obeyed. Again and again, his lips found hers. His hands lifted her gown, and he knew her again. They gave themselves fully to one another, the weight of their transgression drowned out by the fire of their union.

When they were spent, they emerged from the stables, the fading glow of the horizon casting long shadows as day gave way to night.

"I will see you back at the house," Valen said, adjusting his tunic and brushing stray hay from his hair.

Cassia nodded. "I will be there soon, my prince."

They shared a lingering kiss before Valen turned and walked away. Cassia watched him go, her heart pounding—not with love, but with a strange exhilaration that felt both thrilling and dangerous.

Then, she felt it. A prickle at the back of her neck. The unmistakable sensation of being watched.

"Come out, Marcia," she said. "I know you're there."

Marcia stepped hesitantly from behind a tree.

"You need to stop this, Cassia."h

Cassia smirked. "How long have you been there? Judging by the look on your face, I take it you've been hiding there for quite some time. Did you enjoy spying on us? Witnessing our passions of the flesh?"

"This isn't right, Cassia. Repent now and never do this again with Valen."

"Or what?" Cassia took a slow step toward her, her smirk growing darker. "What are you going to do, Marcia?"

"I'm your friend," Marcia said. "I only want what's best for you. I love you."

Cassia spat. "You don't know what love is. You're just a simple girl."

"And what are you?" Marcia asked. "Do you love Valen?"

Cassia scoffed. "Love him? He is mine. Body and soul."

She didn't love Valen—she possessed him. He was hers, as a farmer might own sheep or oxen. He would never leave her, never betray her. In fact, she was certain he would do anything she demanded. That was better than love. Love required vulnerability. Possession was power.

Marcia clasped her hands together over her chest. "I don't even recognize you anymore. I've been praying for you, Cassia, but it seems you've gone too far."

"Save your prayers, Marcia. I don't care for your god."

Marcia's eyes widened. "Jesus Christ, forgive you!"

That name. That loathsome name! Something deep within Cassia twisted and roiled at the sound of it. She stormed toward Marcia and snatched the girl's arm, digging her nails into flesh, drawing a sharp yelp of pain.

"Get in my way again, girl, and I swear you'll regret it!" Cassia hissed.

Marcia's face turned ashen. "L-let go of me!"

Cassia pushed Marcia to the ground. She stood over her, glaring down with cold, unyielding eyes. She should kill the bitch. End her pitiful existence. Let her join her precious Christ in whatever afterlife she prayed for. She could strangle her right there. But then—oh, the wasted blood.

The thought lingered for only a moment before she spun on her heel and stalked away, leaving Marcia to weep.

***

"Bite me. I want you to bite me. Bite my neck."

Valen was inside her, propping her against an outcropping. They were just outside the village at the top of a hill.

He did as she bade him and bit her softly.

"Harder," she moaned.

He did, feeling the tender flesh of her neck tighten against his teeth.

"Even harder, my prince."

And so he did until the skin of her neck split and blood gushed into his mouth, down his throat. She let out a cry of pleasure and hugged him closer to her.

"That's it," she said. "Keep drinking."

Her blood tasted like sweet pomegranates. He drank it as though it were water, sucking the blood from the bite wounds.

"My God!"

A voice exclaimed.

And it belonged to her father.

V

"Papa!" Cassia cried.

Her father stood before her. Beside him was Marcia, her gaze cast downward.

"Valen, what have you done?" Her father's fists were clenched so tightly that his knuckles had turned white.

Cassia had never seen her father like this before. He was a man of calm reason, a beacon of steady faith. But now, his usual composure was shattered. His expression was one of betrayal and righteous fury, and his shoulders were taut.

"I..." Valen faltered. His face paled save for the stark crimson streaks of blood smeared across his lips and chin.

"I saved you. I healed you. I shared my home and my food with you. And this—this is how you repay me?"

Valen wiped at his mouth with the back of his hand, but the crimson stain only spread.

"Is that blood?" Her father looked at her, his eyes narrowing at the bite marks on her neck. "Is this some kind of demonic ritual? Was this your plan all along, Valen? To bring the corruption of Rome and its demons into my house. To my daughter?"

Cassia's heart pounded, her mind racing for an explanation. She glanced at Marcia, who stood frozen, guilt written plainly across her face.

"This was your doing," Cassia spat. "You betrayed me, Marcia. Of course, you did. I should have dealt with you when I found you spying on us. Jealousy—yes, that's it. You're jealous. Jealous that Valen is mine, not yours. That he loves me, not you."

Marcia looked up. "I'm sorry, Cassia."

"Never mind that!" her father barked, his voice snapping like a whip. "Go—now! Fetch cloths from the village, and hurry!"

Marcia nodded, and without another word, she turned and sprinted down the hill toward the village.

"I thought of you as my son."

Valen remained silent, his head bowed in shame. Cassia turned her gaze toward him, waiting—hoping—for him to proclaim his love for her, to stand up for her.

But he said nothing.

So she spoke for him.

"He loves me," she declared.

Her father recoiled. "Loves you? You think this is love? Oh, Cassia..." He tilted his face upward. "Marcia warned me. I'm a fool for not listening to her." His eyes burned as they locked onto hers. "This is not love. Far from it. Now, come here, Cassia."

But she did not move. Instead, she clung to Valen's arm, her grip possessive. "He is mine! All mine!"

Her voice—it was hers, and yet it wasn't.

"Get away from her!" Decimus roared.

He lunged forward, grabbing Cassia by the arm and yanking her toward him. With his other hand, he shoved Valen, the force of it catching the young man off guard.

Valen stumbled backward, his boots scraping against the rocky ground. One step. Two steps. On the third step, his heel caught on a loose stone, and his balance faltered. He staggered, arms flailing, his eyes widening in panic as he realized too late that there was no ground left beneath him.

"Valen!" Cassia reached for him, her fingers outstretched.

Valen's hand shot toward hers, but Decimus's grip on her arm tightened, pulling her back. Their hands missed by mere inches.

Valen's scream pierced the night as he plunged over the cliff's edge.

And then—silence.

Cassia tore free from her father's hold, her heart pounding as she rushed to the edge of the cliff. The sharp wind stung her face as she peered over the precipice.

Below, Valen's broken body lay sprawled across the jagged rocks. His arm and leg were twisted at unnatural angles, and his lifeless eyes stared up at her.

Her father approached, standing beside her. He, too, looked down and saw that Valen was dead. For a brief moment, his face softened.

But it didn't last. His expression darkened. He didn't perform the sign of the cross, didn't utter a prayer for forgiveness.

Instead, he wrapped his arms around Cassia, pulling her away from the edge.

They left Valen's body behind, abandoned to the scavengers.

***

Hours later—Valen awoke.

He gasped, his chest heaving as his eyes snapped open. The first thing he saw was the vast expanse of a star-studded sky above him. The moon hung low and full, its pale, silvery glow casting a light over the scene.

He blinked, disoriented, before sitting up slowly. The aches he expected from his fall never came. Instead, a strange, electric energy coursed through him.

"I'm alive," he murmured. He looked down at his hands, turning them over, studying them in the moonlight. Where his skin had once been bronzed from countless hours under the sun, it was now pale, almost luminous, reflecting the moonlight in an unearthly way.

Something was different. Something powerful.

His throat burned, dry as the sand of a desert, and his stomach churned with an ache that gnawed at him from the inside. Hunger. No, not just hunger—ravenous need.

Instinctively, he wet his lips, and he tasted something faintly sweet and metallic. Blood. Cassia's blood. It had dried on his lips, but the taste ignited something deep within him.

He froze as his tongue brushed against something sharp. With his hand, he traced over the edges of his teeth. Fangs. Long, pointed, deadly fangs.

He wasn't simply alive. He was...changed.

The burning in his throat intensified, consuming his thoughts. He clenched his hands into fists, his nails digging into his palms as he tried to will the need away. But it was useless. His entire body screamed for relief, for sustenance.

For blood.

VI

Cassia finally fell asleep. She had cried until her eyes were raw and red, sobbing until her body surrendered to exhaustion. Decimus sat beside her, watching her chest rise and fall with the steady rhythm of slumber.

She had gone through so much. Did she love Valen? No. It wasn't love. How could it be? Perhaps it wasn't even lust. There was something far darker beneath the surface. The wounds on her neck—those vile bite marks—confirmed as much. Even the way she had spoken had been unnatural. It was as though she hadn't been herself at all.

A demon. He had seen priests cast out demons before, just as Christ Himself had done. But Decimus was no exorcist. He lacked the training, the knowledge, the courage. He had never encountered a demon personally, though he had seen the demon dogs that the Roman soldiers kept, their eyes glowing with an unholy light.

Was that what he faced now? Was his own daughter...possessed?

And if she was, what was he to do? Should he call upon a priest trained in the rites of exorcism? Or perhaps even a demon slayer, those holy warriors who wielded their black swords?

What if it wasn't over?

He gently brushed a strand of hair from Cassia's face. She looked so much like her mother. How had it come to this? How had he allowed his daughter to stray so far? He loved her, didn't he? Of course, he did. But wasn't it a father's duty to protect his child?

Lord Jesus Christ, Son of God, have mercy.

Time would heal her wounds, both physical and spiritual. He would watch over her, keep her close, and ensure that her condition, whatever it was, didn't worsen. Agrippa and Dosia's wedding would have to wait. So would the final preparations for the church. Even his ministry would have to pause—for now. And yet, deep down, he feared that time alone would not be enough. If Cassia showed more signs of demonic possession, then he would have no choice but to summon someone more capable.

But the thought of calling upon a priest or a demon slayer made his heart shiver. Cassia wasn't the only one suffering spiritually. Decimus felt the weight of his own sin like a stone tied to his soul.

Murder. He was a murderer.

Tears stung his eyes, and he buried his face in his hands.

"Lord Jesus Christ, Son of God, have mercy on me, a sinner."

He said the words, but they felt hollow. What scared him most wasn't his guilt or even the dark presence that seemed to haunt his daughter.

What terrified him was the quiet, shameful truth he couldn't admit aloud: he was glad Valen was gone. He was glad the boy lay dead at the bottom of the plateau, broken and lifeless.

And for that, Decimus feared there might be no mercy for him at all.

***

"Papa! Papa, wake up!"

Decimus jolted awake. Cassia's tear-streaked face loomed above him.

"Cassia?" he gasped, sitting up and pulling her closer. "What's wrong? You're shaking!"

She wasn't just shaking; she was convulsing. Her eyes were wide with fear.

"P-papa," she stammered, her voice broken and raw. "I...I'm sorry... Please...take it away from me..."

Decimus wrapped his arms around her, holding her tightly, his protective instincts roaring to life. She buried her face in his chest, her sobs muffled but wrenching.

"Shhh," he whispered, stroking her back in soothing circles as he had when she was a baby. "I'm here, Cassia. I'm here."

Her body was cold; frigid, like she had been standing in the icy depths of a river. The chill seeped into his own skin.

"You're so cold," he said. "What happened?"

Cassia gripped his arms tighter. "D-don't let t-them get me, p-papa! Please!"

Her terror was palpable. He leaned back to look into her eyes, his brow furrowing as he cupped her face.

"Who, Cassia? Who's trying to get you?"

Her words came out in fragmented gasps. "N-not dead. H-he's not d-dead."

A shadow unfurled in his chest.

Valen.

It wasn't possible. He had seen Valen's corpse at the bottom of the cliff. But the dread in Cassia's eyes spoke volumes. If what she said was true, then something unnatural had happened.

A demon. He truly was a demon. And he wanted Cassia.

"I won't let him have you," Decimus said. "We will stop him. I promise you, God will protect us."

"H-how?"

Calling on a demon slayer or an exorcist would take time they didn't have. They needed immediate sanctuary.

"The church," he said. "A demon cannot enter a house of the Lord. We'll go there."

"What if—" Cassia began, but Decimus cut her off, his hand firm on her shoulder.

"We will gather the others. We will pray. Together, we will drive this evil out."

VII

Harsh winds battered the ancient stone walls of the temple. These were not ordinary winds. Each time the winds buffeted the walls, an eerie wailing could be heard, as though from tormented spirits.

"He's coming, Father," Dosia said. Fear was clear on her face, as it was on the others.

Decimus took a steadying breath, though fear gripped his own heart like a vice. He could not show it. He was their priest, their shepherd, their spiritual father. It was his duty to guide and protect them. Even now. Especially now.

"Keep praying," he urged. Dosia, Agrippa, Marcia, and Fabian—all of them had gathered in the dim glow of candlelight. They were his faithful congregation, his flock. "Just as I taught you," he said, moving among them. "Pray without ceasing. He cannot enter God's house. Such evil is not permitted."

He wanted to believe his own words.

Cassia stood apart from the others, her arms wrapped around herself. Her face was pale, her eyes red-rimmed from tears shed.

"I won't let anything happen to you, Cassia," he said to her. "I promise."

Candles illuminated the chamber in a soft, golden glow, while narrow beams of moonlight pierced through the high, narrow openings in the stone. The heavy wooden gate was bolted shut, reinforced with a sliding beam. Icons of the Virgin Mary and John the Baptist hung on the walls. On the dais stood a simple wooden cross.

Decimus shook. He clenched his hands into fists, willing the trembling to stop.

"Lord Jesus Christ, Son of God, have mercy on us," he whispered under his breath.

He looked at each of them—Dosia, strong but frightened; Marcia, quietly weeping in prayer; Fabian, pale and wide-eyed; and Agrippa, clutching his bride's hand tightly. His gaze returned to Cassia, who stared at the flickering candles, her face unreadable.

His own fear was suffocating. He did not want to die.

He was a priest. He believed in eternal life through Christ. And yet, even so, the thought of death terrified him.

A howling whoosh swept through the temple, extinguishing all the candles in an instant. Darkness enveloped them, broken only by the baleful light of the moon. But this was no ordinary darkness. It was alive with a malevolent presence. Something sinister coiled in the shadows, vile and otherworldly. Demonic.

Decimus felt it in his very bones.

"Don't stop praying," he urged. "Keep praying!"

May the Lord have mercy. May the Lord have mercy.

The sound came suddenly—*BANG!* A deafening impact against the temple gate. It wasn't a knock. It was a forceful, violent smash.

Lord, have mercy. Lord, have mercy. Lord, have mercy.

The pounding came again and again. The gate rattled with each strike. The wooden bolt groaned under the strain.

Lord-have-mercy! Lord-have-mercy! Lord-have-mercy!

CRACK!

Another tremendous blow split the bolt. The gate swung open, slamming against the walls.

A dense gray mist poured into the temple, carrying a scent of decay. It slithered across the floor like a living thing, climbing the walls and swirling around the dais.

And from within the mist, a figure emerged.

Dressed in black, he stepped forward with an abnormal grace, the mist parting around him. His long black hair framed a pale face that looked as though it had been carved from alabaster. His lips were a rich vermilion, unnaturally vibrant, and parted just enough to reveal two gleaming fangs.

His eyes—violet and hypnotic—fixed on Decimus and then on Cassia.

It was Valen.

Back from the dead.

Decimus stepped forward, his knees threatening to buckle beneath him. "Fear not," he said. "The Lord is with us. He will save us."

But as he spoke, the mist surged upward, sweeping over the icons on the walls. When it receded, dark stains remained, marring the holy images, as though to blind the figures of the Virgin Mary and John the Baptist.

Valen ambled towards them, his booted steps echoing. “I’ve come for my bride,” he said, his voice like the gentle rustle of silk against bare skin. He held his hand out, his fingernails long and pointed. “Cassia.”

Cassia, her wide, bloodshot eyes locked on Valen’s, began to step forward, as though drawn by an invisible chain.

“Don’t move, Cassia! Stay where you are!” Decimus glared at Valen, a whisper of bravery spiking inside of him. “I won’t let you have her!”

Valen smirked. “Your god cannot save you now, Father.”

Decimus seized the wooden cross from the dais and held it aloft. “Begone from here, demon!”

Valen’s expression turned curious, as if regarding a child waving a toy sword. And then, with no more effort than a tilt of his head, the wooden cross began to twist. Its once-pristine lines warped into a deformed shape, blackened as though consumed by fire.

Decimus stumbled back, staring in horror at what had been his shield of faith. “W-what...? Oh, God...”

In a flash, Valen clutched Decimus’s throat and lifted the priest clear off the floor. Decimus’s legs kicked helplessly as he struggled to break free. But Valen’s grip was iron, cutting off Decimus’s air.

Valen scowled. “Too late, Father. Give me what is mine.”

And with a flick of his wrist, he snapped Decimus’s neck.

ACT TWO

I

The temple stood in serene isolation, its limestone facade weathered from the passage of time. Vines and moss grew along the fluted columns and a single withered tree leaned toward the entrance, its leafless branches undulating in the afternoon breeze, its roots curling over ancient stones.

"Many years ago, this temple once belonged to Absalona," Carpus said, "the Goddess of Blood. Many worshiped her here, spilling their own blood as an offering."

He stood near his mule, bags of his belongings packed and slung over the mule's back. He patted the animal gently, calming her nerves, for he wasn't the only one who sensed the terrifying aura emanating from the temple. It was nearly palpable.

"Was there human sacrifice?" the traveler asked him.

"Not that I know of. Absalona is a goddess of blood, not death. It was a kind of ritualistic bloodletting."

"I see."

Carpus swallowed hard. He had fulfilled his task: meeting the traveler near the city of Iader and leading him to the temple. Surely, that was enough. He was abandoning his village and his farm. All of it left behind in exchange for a chance at survival. Whatever cursed blight had seized the village, it had spiraled into something far worse than death.

But this traveler—could he truly save them? He certainly looked the part of a warrior, with a strange black sword at his side. It was darker than any metal Carpus had seen, its edge seeming to absorb the sunlight rather than reflect it. The traveler's attire was equally somber: black leather armor, sturdy boots, and a billowing black cloak. He was perhaps thirty years old with a shadow of a beard. He had sharp and refined features, an olive complexion, and striking, sky-blue eyes.

Perhaps this traveler was one of those demon slayers he had heard about. Jupiter knew the village could use the aid of such warriors.

But could one single demon slayer stop that which plagued their village?

Doubtful. Highly doubtful. Good thing Carpus was leaving. The rest could rot for all he cared.

"What happened to the temple?" the traveler asked. His voice was smooth and clear, though it carried a melancholic weight.

"A priest by the name of Decimus took it over," Carpus said. "He cleared out all the remnants of Absalona and replaced them with his own god. Chris-something?"

"Jesus Christ," the traveler supplied.

"That's the one." Carpus cleared his throat and spat onto the dirt trail. They were still at a safe distance from the foreboding temple. He had no intention of getting any closer. "Decimus had a small following. He was a good man, I suppose."

Good man, yes—but reckless. Stupid, even. To meddle with gods and demons and their temples was to court death.

"Was?"

The traveler knew so little. Was this part of Carpus's task, too? To elucidate the man? Well, he had no inclination for that.

"He died," he said, simply. "Killed not long ago."

Something quivered in the temple's darkened openings—a smoky, ash-colored figure, there one moment and gone the next.

Carpus flinched. His skin prickled, and his grip on the mule's reins tightened.

"Is something wrong?" the traveler asked.

"N-no. Well..." Carpus looked again at the opening but saw nothing. He darted nervous glances around him. Finally, he leaned closer to the traveler and lowered his voice. "They say this place is haunted by evil spirits. You can hear their shrill cries all the way back to our village on some nights. No one's dared set foot inside since the day Decimus died."

"A demon, perhaps."

Carpus chuckled nervously. "Many demons exist in these parts."

The traveler nodded, then started toward the temple's gated entrance.

"Where are you going?"

"Inside. I was sent here for a reason, and I intend to find out what that is."

Fool. Were all these Christ followers so eager for death?

"Aren't you afraid?"

The traveler stopped and turned back to Carpus. He flashed a wry smile, then faced forward and continued on to the temple.

Carpus exhaled heavily, shaking his head. "Brave or foolish, I don't know," he muttered. "And I don't care, either."

He adjusted the straps on his mule, ensuring his belongings were secure, then tugged the reins. The mule brayed softly, and together they started down the path. Carpus didn't know where he was going. Anywhere but here would do. All that mattered was putting as much distance as possible between himself and that cursed temple.

II

"Well, my boy," rasped the demon in Andreas's mind, *"it's not every day we get to visit a desecrated temple."*

Andras the Deathchaser, the demon bound to Andreas's soul, was a constant presence. Unlike with most possessions, Andreas had gained self-control after years of training at Mount Athos. Though the Deathchaser whispered, taunted, and occasionally offered counsel, he could do little without Andreas's consent.

Andreas stood at the threshold of the ancient temple. Its entrance gate, a massive wooden structure reinforced with iron, hung askew. The wood was splintered and cracked, and the iron was warped as though struck repeatedly with a battering ram.

"What do you know of this goddess?" Andreas asked the demon inside him. There were few benefits to harboring a demon, but knowledge of the macabre of Hades was certainly one of them.

"Absalona? First time I'm hearing of her. She must have been a lowly demon if she let a simple priest take over her temple. Who knows? Perhaps she wasn't a demon at all."

"What else could she be?" he asked.

"A fiend."

Fiends weren't quite demons, though they came from them. They were the deformed, chaos abominations of the demonic. Like demons, fiends twisted the very thing that made all mankind good and normal. In some cases, fiends were the manifestation of gruesome sin. It was believed that Saul, the first king of Israel, had become a fiend in the form of a ghastly wraith.

But there was something darker here. Far darker than any fiend. Andreas felt the dread of a demonic presence. Or at least the remnants of that presence.

A demon had been here. And recently.

Andreas had received this summons from the bishops of Mount Athos. Little had been known of it. All Andreas was told was to meet a farmer named Carpus on the road to Iader, and that Carpus would take him to his destination. Having been summoned, Andreas had journeyed through a portal in the unseen realm, a means through which demon slayers and priests traveled quickly through the Roman Empire, and had met with Carpus.

"Well, my boy, what are you waiting for? Go on in."

And so he did.

Inside the temple were the clear signs of a great struggle. Icons had been torn down. Wooden crosses had been broken in two. The remains of the gate's lock lay in pieces in a corner, already covered in spiderwebs.

But the clearest sign was the corpse that lay on the stone floor.

"This must be the priest. Or was the priest, I should say. Seems he's been dead for some time."

Andreas knelt down next to the corpse. The skin was near translucent, the lips blue, the eyes red and strained in horror, the veins visible in sickening black and purple.

But something was off.

"No blood..."

In fact, there was no sign of a wound at all. Except—

He caught sight of markings on the corpse's neck. Gently, he turned the head to the side, exposing what looked like a bite mark from two very sharp fangs.

Had someone sucked the blood from the priest?

Was this Absalona's doing? If indeed she was a goddess of blood, surely this was part of some ritual.

A soft, mournful sound issued, and the hairs on Andreas's neck stood on end. The sound lingered, fading in and out.

There was a presence, too. Not demonic, but cold nonetheless. As cold as the corpse that lay before him.

"My boy, we're not alone in here."

Andreas got to his feet and drew the black sword from his belt. The sword was a lahat chereb—flame of the whirling sword—that all demon slayers carried. It was a version of the sword the cherubim protecting the gates to Eden carried. An extremely deadly weapon, especially to demons and their fiends.

"Are you a demon slayer?"

An echoing voice. But not the voice of a demon.

"I am," Andreas answered, searching everywhere but seeing nothing.

"Thank the Lord you have come."

"Who are you?" Andreas kept his guard up. "Show yourself."

"I'm over here."

Andreas turned in the direction of the voice and still saw nothing.

Then his gaze narrowed as something faded into being, a shadow torn from the fabric of the unseen realm.

A ghost, and one that shared the likeness of the priest's corpse.

III

"My name is Decimus, and when I was alive I was a priest."

The pallid ghost of Decimus floated through the desolated temple, its form ever-shifting, as though woven from threads of mist. The air around the spirit seemed to quiver, and he was draped in a tattered cloak of light gray.

It was not the first time Andreas had encountered a ghost, though most of the spirits he encountered were the fiends of demons known as wraiths.

"Was it you who called for me?" he asked, sheathing his black sword.

"Not quite," Decimus said. "I had one of the members of my church summon for you. She managed to escape before being turned."

Andreas frowned. "Turned?"

Decimus drifted toward his corpse, moving with a kind of eerie grace. He looked down at himself. "It's hard to see one's corpse, especially when it has been so defiled."

"Tell me what happened."

Decimus looked at Andreas and his ghostly eyes were full of both anger and fear. "My blood was sucked from my veins. Every last drop."

"A vampire."

The ghost nodded.

Like wraiths, vampires were demonic fiends that fed on the blood of their mortal victims. Demons fashioned vampires from mankind, feeding them demonic blood. Vampires were near immortal and had aetheric powers similar to the demon that had turned them. Some vampires were said to have lived for hundreds of years, even before the time of Christ.

But if a vampire had done this, then someone must have made that vampire, and only a demon could do that.

"I was born and raised in Iader," Decimus explained, "and I came to know Christ through a group of traveling priests. They taught me all that I know and I journeyed with them for a time, learning from them, helping them spread the Gospel. I became a priest, met my wife, and we had a daughter, Cassia. Unfortunately, my wife died soon after giving birth."

"I'm sorry."

Decimus nodded. "Thank you. Soon after my wife died, I started a church. I knew of this temple. It had been abandoned several years back. I cleaned it and decorated it with my own handmade icons and crosses." Those icons were now marked with black stains and the crosses were twisted and bent. "It was a small church. Many of the villagers were not interested in the Lord, but some were. I loved each of them as though they were my own family."

"Quite self-righteous, this priest is. Holier than thou, eh, my boy?"

Andreas ignored the demon in his mind. He asked Decimus, "And the vampire?"

"Valen is his name. He was a Roman soldier. A deserter. A young boy, far too young to be fighting in battles. I found him passed out, wounded and near death. He had come from the far north. I healed him and gave him a place to stay. But he betrayed me. Took everything from me, including my life."

"He must have done something to anger the boy-vampire."

Though Andreas made no indication, he had to agree with the Deathchaser. This Valen must have had some reason to betray the priest. The reason might not necessarily have been a good one, but something had provoked him.

"And your daughter?" Andreas asked. "What of her?"

"He took her. Took her before he became a vampire and took her now. I don't know what's become of her."

Inside his mind, Andras chuckled. *"Ah, and there it is. Seems Valen took the poor girl's purity, and our preachy preacher was none too pleased with that carnal development."*

"And how did Valen become a vampire?"

"I don't know."

In this, Andreas believed him, but there was something the ghostly priest was holding back from telling him. As much as he hated to admit that Andras was right, Decimus did have an air of self-piety to him, not at all like the other priests Andreas knew, who were testaments to true humility.

Then again, Decimus had been killed in a most gruesome way and his killer had taken his daughter captive, and, judging by his story, all Decimus had wanted was to help those in need.

For all Andreas knew, Decimus's self-righteousness was, perhaps, warranted.

"You seek revenge?" Andreas asked.

"No," Decimus was quick to say. Too quick, in fact. He wrung his hands together. "Well, yes. But that is not all. I want you to save my daughter and the village. Valen has them under his control, feeding on the villagers like they're cattle. I fear what has happened to my daughter. Perhaps it is too late for her. Perhaps he has already turned her."

Either the daughter had been turned or killed the same as Decimus. Yet the evidence suggested she was still alive, as it seemed this Valen was embittered by Decimus but in love with Cassia. Perhaps Decimus had forbidden Valen from seeing her and Valen had resorted to using sinister forces.

"This Valen sold his soul for love. How romantic."

Love? No. This was anything but love. Lust, obsession, passion—all of which paved the way to Hades.

"If he has turned your daughter," Andreas said, "there may still be hope for her. If the vampire who turned her is slain, the effects of the vampirism may be reversed."

Decimus's eyes widened. "Truly? Oh, thank the Lord!"

"I said *may* be reversed. I've never seen it done."

"But there's hope?"

Andreas nodded. Mortals who were turned into vampires were, strictly speaking, dead, but their souls were trapped in their bodies, keeping them in a kind of life but hungry for the life force of all mankind—blood. Reversing the vampirism meant freeing the shackles that held the soul trapped, but it didn't always mean the soul would remain to animate the body.

In some cases, the body expired and the soul was taken to Paradise or to Hades.

"That is what I need now most of all. Thank you, demon slayer."

"So a vampire is all we have to contend with? Simple. Fiends are no match for you, my boy."

But we still don't know who changed Valen, Andreas thought, knowing the demon could hear his thoughts. He rarely made it known that he harbored a demon inside of him, for such was near comical for a demon slayer. Normally, demon slayers had a guardian angel by their side. *Perhaps it was this Absalona.*

"A mere annoyance. A lowly demon is less than dirt compared to my strength."

And where all demon slayers relied on the aetheric power of their guardian angels, Andreas was a special case, relying on the dark aether of Andras.

"Then I leave for the village," Andreas said, turning around.

"Wait."

Andreas stopped and looked back at the ghost. With his task relayed to him, it made sense for the priest to ascend to Paradise.

"I want to go with you. I need to see my daughter one last time. I need to make sure she is safe."

"Your place now is in Paradise, Decimus. Leave this to me."

"No."

The tone was hard, the word sharp.

Andreas paused.

"Please," Decimus said. "I still have time. I need to make this right."

Make what right? Perhaps on their way to the village he could probe Decimus for more answers. Doubtless, he hadn't been forthcoming with all the details. There was more, Andreas was sure, and he would find out what it was.

As for time—since Decimus had lost his life recently, then he did have time yet before ascending to Paradise. All souls had forty days before either being accepted into Paradise to get a foretaste of the glories of the new Heaven and the new earth or getting thrown into Hades to get a foretaste of the torturous Lake of Fire, all before the Final Judgment of the Lord God.

"Please."

Andreas had no reason to deny him. "If that is your wish, I suppose I can't stop you."

Decimus let out a sigh, and his shoulders sagged. "Thank you."

"Let us be off, then."

Again, Andreas turned to make his way out of the temple.

"One more thing," Decimus said.

And again, Andreas stopped, turning back to Decimus. "And that is?" He hid his annoyance poorly.

Decimus breezed past Andreas and halted at the threshold of the temple's entrance. The priest pointed outside.

"That."

He pointed at strange purple and red clouds, black lightning, and falling ashes.

And demons.

Lots of demons.

IV

Andreas counted more than two dozen demons circling the chaotic skies. Their skeletal wings sliced through the air as chains rattled and clanged against their decayed, ghastly forms. Their faces resembled those of vultures, with empty, soulless eyes.

These were scavenger demons of the unseen realm. They feasted on the souls of the departed, carrying them to the dark, tormenting depths of Hades.

At the moment a person's soul departed their body, both demons and angels gathered. The battle for the soul depended on the life lived. If the person had died in sin, unrepentant and unreconciled to God the Father, the scavenger demons claimed them. But for those who had accepted Jesus Christ as their Savior and Healer, the angels of Heaven would lift their souls into Paradise.

And yet, here in this accursed place, Andreas saw no angels.

"Is this why you never left the temple?" Andreas asked.

"Yes," Decimus admitted. "I sanctified this place years ago. Despite its desecration, it retains a fragment of its holiness. The demons fear to enter and take my soul."

"But where are the angels?" Andreas questioned. Not a single angelic figure appeared among the demons. Not even Decimus's guardian angel.

Decimus was alone in death.

"Forsaken is more like it, my boy."

"Angels should be here for your soul as well," Andreas said. "Why aren't they? Are you not repentant? Are you not truly of the faithful?"

At this, Decimus clearly took offense. "Of course, I am! I gave my life to the Lord!"

And yet, the absence of angels raised troubling questions. None of this made sense. If Decimus had lived as a follower of Jesus, if he had truly repented, one angel would have been enough to fend off any number of scavenger demons. It wasn't a matter of strength—it was divine authority. Angels didn't hesitate to claim the righteous.

This complicated matters.

"Away with you, demon slayer!" one of the scavenger demons squawked. "His soul is ours! He belongs to us!"

Andreas stepped out from under the shadow of the temple. The ash-filled wind slapped against his face and cloak, carrying the acrid stench of burning flesh. The very air seemed to rebel against nature, thick and suffocating, swirling with malevolence.

Ash rained from the churning, unnatural clouds above, a telltale sign of decreation. Where the divine worked to create and sustain life, demons brought chaos and reversed creation itself. That was what left the weather and the environment in such disarray.

"I will not let you take him," Andreas said, his voice cold.

"Do you truly intend to fight them all?" Decimus asked.

Andreas didn't respond with words. Instead, he drew his lahat chereb. The demons screeched and wailed from above, their chains rattling like a foreboding death knell.

"You are but one man, demon slayer," one of the demons sneered, its vulture-like head tilting. "You cannot hope to succeed against us."

"We shall see."

With a deep breath, he summoned the sword's aether. Holy, blue flames erupted along the length of the blade. The flames were no ordinary fire; they burned with divine purpose, capable of incinerating the essence of anything demonic. But the fire was a double-edged sword—it seared Andreas as well, starting at the palms of his hands and spreading up his arms in agonizing waves.

The holy fire fought against Andras, the demon bound within him. The longer Andreas wielded the flames, the greater the risk they would consume him entirely.

The scavenger demons screeched in rage, and several dove toward him with terrifying speed. They came like hawks to a worm.

But Andreas was no easy prey.

He slashed upward with his blade, unleashing an arc of blue fire that tore through the air. The flames reached the diving demons before they could react, enveloping them in a torrent of divine destruction. Their shrieks of pain and fury were silenced in an instant as the fire consumed them utterly. Not even a trace of ash remained.

The remaining scavenger demons cursed and hissed, circling warily in the sky above. But none dared approach the temple again. Instead, they beat their skeletal wings furiously and fled, disappearing into the darkened horizon.

As the demons fled, the environment gradually returned to normal. The clouds dissipated like vapor, revealing patches of blue sky. The strange ash rain ceased. And the harsh wind softened into a gentle, soothing breeze.

"Remarkable..." Decimus said as he watched the transformation in awe.

"Some escaped," Andreas said, sheathing his lahat chereb. "They will bring others. You knew this would happen, didn't you?"

"I did. I nearly lost my soul once when I left the temple."

Andreas frowned. "The scavengers of Hades won't stop. They'll hunt us until they have your soul."

"I have a solution," Decimus said. "If I may..."

Andreas gestured for him to continue.

"There's a reason I called for you specifically. You're Andreas of Mount Athos, the demon slayer who fights demons by harboring a demon himself."

Andreas tensed slightly, the notoriety unsettling him. He couldn't decide if he was famous or infamous.

"The latter, my boy. Definitely the latter," Andras's sardonic voice chimed in his mind.

"What of it?" Andreas said, his tone clipped.

Decimus looked directly at him, his spectral gaze steady. "Let me possess your body."

In Andreas's mind, the Deathchaser sighed. *"Interesting..."*

Andreas shook his head. "I have enough voices in my head."

"I only seek shelter inside your body and mind. The scavenger demons cannot sense me there."

"It is doable," Andras supplemented. *"Though hosting the soul of the departed is no easy feat. It will drain your aether and limit your abilities."*

"There has to be another way," Andreas said, frustration edging his voice as he addressed Decimus. "This—this is reckless."

"It's the only way to keep me hidden," Decimus urged.

"Let him come inside, my boy."

You can't be serious.

"Deadly serious. I don't trust this priest either, but if he's inside you, it means I'll have access to him. I'll uncover what he's hiding. Besides, he's right—this will keep the scavengers off our trail."

Andreas studied the ghostly priest. The proposition held undeniable advantages, but the risks were equally apparent. Hosting another soul would sap his strength, and he had no way of gauging just how much.

So much for a simple summons to slay a vampire. This had become a labyrinth of unforeseen complications.

Still, did he really have a choice?

"Very well," Andreas said. "I accept your proposal."

Decimus's spectral form brightened. "You do? Thank you! Truly, you are a man of God!" He floated closer. "Forgive me, but I'm not entirely certain how to do this. I'll try my best."

Andreas steeled himself for what was to come. "Do what you must."

The priest reached a hand out and pressed into Andreas's chest. The icy touch sent a jolt through Andreas. He caught his breath as the unexpected cold spread through his torso. The instinct to shove Decimus away surged within him—

But it was too late.

The ghost passed through him, fully and completely, moving as if he were nothing more than mist.

Andreas's head snapped back. He cried out as his entire body convulsed. The sensation was overwhelming; foreign yet hauntingly familiar. It was like the day Andras had possessed him. His knees buckled, and he collapsed onto the ground, his chest heaving as nausea churned in his stomach.

Seconds passed like hours. Then the sickness ebbed, leaving only the faint chill of Decimus's presence lingering in his core. Andreas took a moment to steady his breathing before finally forcing himself to stand.

"Are you there, Decimus?" Andreas asked.

"I'm here."

The priest's voice echoed in his mind in the same way that Andras spoke to him. The possession had worked. Strange, though, that Decimus's presence brought no soothing warmth, no sense of divine grace or holiness. Instead, his soul felt just as dark and cold as the Deathchaser's.

"Good," Andreas muttered. "Direct me to your village."

The weight of three souls within him was something altogether new. It wasn't just the sensation of Decimus's consciousness pressing against his own—there was more. His aether was slipping, draining like a slow trickle of water from a fractured vessel.

V

When Decimus entered Andreas's body, he was enveloped by a void of darkness so complete it felt suffocating. But then, as though waking from a vivid dream, he found himself in a meadow that stretched endlessly in all directions. The ground was blanketed in flowers with black petals, their delicate forms swaying in a gentle breeze that carried a strangely pleasant scent.

He looked down at himself and found that he appeared as he had been in life—dressed in his simple robe and sandals. To his surprise, he felt solid, corporeal, as though he had been fully restored.

Above, the sky was an expanse of unbroken blue, with no clouds in sight. Even the sun was present in this space, its warm rays cascading over the surreal landscape. It was tranquil; a place of quietude and stillness that any priest or monk would find perfect for meditative prayer and communion with the Lord Jesus Christ.

"Is this inside the demon slayer's mind?" he wondered aloud.

"Finally, some company!"

An unsettling voice cut through the calm.

The voice didn't seem to come from any single direction. It was everywhere at once: above, below, to his left, to his right.

"Who's there?" he demanded.

A figure materialized in front of him. The being had the face of a black owl with piercing scarlet eyes. His body was cloaked in a flowing black cloak that billowed even in the gentle wind. Tucked behind his shoulders were black, feathery wings.

"You didn't think you'd be inside Andreas alone, did you?" the figure said.

Decimus stepped back. "You're the demon that possesses him."

But was this a demon? There was something majestic about his bearing. Angelic, even.

Was this what a fallen angel looked like?

He shuddered.

"I am a demon prince, the Deathchaser. But you may call me Andras."

Andras. The name was disturbingly close to Andreas.

"Is this some sick joke?"

"It is not, I'm afraid," Andras replied smoothly. "Andreas and I have much in common—not only our names. But enough about me. I want to learn about you, dear Decimus."

The owl head managed a macabre smile.

Decimus resisted the overwhelming urge to scream for help. But help from whom? No one could reach him here.

Perhaps he had gotten far more than he bargained for. Hadn't Andreas claimed to have control over the demon? That was what Decimus had learned about the demon slayer of Mount Athos; that his faith allowed him to subdue the darkness within. But now, looking into those blazing scarlet eyes, doubt crept in.

"You would have overheard my conversations with Andreas," Decimus said, deflecting. "There is nothing more for you to know."

"Oh, I don't believe that's true," Andras said, strolling towards him. "Besides, you are in my domain now, priest."

"Your...domain?" he repeated, a lump forming in his throat.

Andras stopped, fixing him with an amused look. "Do you know what a Circle of Hades is?" Decimus couldn't bring himself to speak and shook his head instead. The demon sighed, as though explaining such things were beneath him.

"A Circle of Hades," Andras began, his voice taking on a lecturing quality, "is a fragment of the unseen realm—the realm of demons, angels, and the Most High, Adonai, Himself. It is a place where the natural laws of the mortal world do not apply. Within a Circle of Hades, I reign supremely. Here, I am both lord and savior."

Andras spread his arms wide, as if to encompass the infinite meadow around them. "This—my entire possession of Andreas—is my Circle of Hades. It is a part of me, and I am its master. To maintain it takes quite a bit of effort, to be honest." His piercing eyes narrowed. "And now that you are inside Andreas, you too are trapped within my Circle of Hades."

The tranquil meadow suddenly felt oppressive, the blue skies above more like a prison ceiling.

"Why are you telling me this?"

"Because, priest," Andras said, stepping closer until he was mere inches from Decimus, "I want you to understand just how powerless you are here."

VI

"I have nothing more to tell," Decimus said.

In the black meadow, Andras began circling him like a wolf stalking its prey. Each step the demon took caused the flowers beneath him to wither and die, only to spring back to life once he moved away.

"Oh, I hardly believe that, my dear Decimus. Tell me, why were there no angels to come take your soul to Paradise?"

"I don't know," Decimus lied. The demon could likely sense his deceit, but he refused to give him anything more. The secrets of his soul were not for this demon, nor were they necessary for Andreas to accomplish his mission.

Andras tilted his head, studying Decimus. "I sense a deep, dark secret within you. And I intend to bring it out into the open, even if I have to drag it kicking and screaming."

"I am a man of God," Decimus countered.

"And you're also a man," Andras replied smoothly. "Which means you are not immune to sin. Even a grave sin."

Decimus's throat clamped shut. He swallowed, then cleared his throat. The black meadow felt so real, as though he were alive again, flesh and blood and utterly vulnerable. But he had to be strong. Andras couldn't harm him; Andreas wouldn't allow it.

He had to believe that.

"I will not confess my sins to the likes of you," Decimus said.

"What? You mean to a demon such as myself? Come now, Father. Who knows sin better than a demon? If that vampire wanted your daughter, he could have taken her easily. Vampires are very good at seducing their victims."

"Cassia had faith in Christ protecting her."

Andras rolled his eyes dramatically. "You kept her from him. They were lovers."

"I protected her!" Decimus snapped. The words burst out before he could stop them. He hated Andras in that moment, and he hoped the demon could see it in his eyes.

Andras, however, remained calm, his demeanor unshaken. "The vampire wanted to kill you. Why?"

"Does a fiend need a reason?"

Andras grunted, clearly unconvinced. "Very well, priest. Keep your secrets. But know that God always finds a way to bring them out into His light."

The demon turned away and walked a few paces forward.

"What are you doing?" Decimus asked warily.

Turning his head just enough to cast a sidelong glance, Andras replied, "You want to see what Andreas sees, don't you?"

With a swipe of his hand through the air, a blurry image began to form. Slowly, it sharpened, revealing the village Decimus had once called home.

"There," Andras said as he lowered himself to the ground. He sat cross-legged, the once-vivid flowers around him dissolving into blackened dirt and mud. Patting the ground beside him, he beckoned with a wicked grin. "Come, come. Sit, sit."

***

Andreas took in the gruesome sight before him: corpses impaled on tall, wooden stakes. Each stake had skewered its victim through their genitals and emerged from their throats, chests, or stomachs. Men and women, old and young alike, hung lifelessly in a horrific display. Yet, curiously, not a single drop of blood stained the ground below them. It was as if their bodies had been drained dry before the stakes had finished their grim work.

"My God," Decimus said in his mind. *"This is a gruesome sight."*

Indeed, it was. The impaled bodies loomed at the edge of the village, a macabre warning meant to terrify and deter. Above, vultures circled lazily. Swarms of flies buzzed, clinging to the rotting flesh.

Andreas reached for the silver cross hanging around his neck. The cross was more than a symbol of his faith; it was a gift from Emidius's daughter, Lucia, a woman he had loved and lost. His fingers tightened around it as he whispered, "Lord Jesus Christ, Son of God, have mercy."

"They were drained of their blood before impalement," said the Deathchaser. *"This reeks of the handiwork of more than one vampire."*

Andreas had suspected as much. No single vampire could have fed on so many victims in such a short span of time.

"I fear there may be more vampires than just Valen at work here," Decimus said. *"But he is the source of this evil."*

"Do you recognize any of them?" Andreas asked.

"I do. And I will pray for them."

Andras's voice came again, harsher this time. *"It's too late for them, priest. Their souls are damned to Hades."*

"If I pray, the Lord will have mercy."

"These were sinners," Andras sneered. *"Valen and his little blood-drinkers did your God a favor. Trust me on that."*

Andreas interrupted, his tone sharp. "Are you two getting along?"

Andras chuckled darkly. *"I've been the perfect host—serving wine and watermelon."*

"Decimus?" Andreas asked, ignoring the demon's sarcasm.

"I'm all right. Don't concern yourself with me. Let us finish this, so no more lives may be lost."

Overhead, the vultures cawed.

Andreas had expected to see panic in the village. Instead, the scene was eerily still. Too still. On the surface, life carried on as if nothing was amiss. Farmers worked in their fields. Mothers clung to their children, keeping them close but not scurrying as one might in the face of danger. Yet, there was a pervasive tension in the air.

No one met Andreas's gaze. Villagers averted their eyes, their heads bowed as he passed. It wasn't just avoidance—it was fear.

Though the village's activities were routine, a grim pall shrouded everything. Farmers' faces were drawn and gaunt, their eyes darting nervously toward the shadows. The mothers who clutched their children worked to keep their composure.

And yet, Andreas saw no signs of vampires. Stranger still, he sensed no demonic presence. It was almost as though the evil here had concealed itself entirely. Or worse, had become a part of the village's daily rhythm.

A sudden shout shattered the uneasy quiet. "Repent! Join our masters of the night! Repent!"

The voice rang out from the village agora. Villagers gathered around a man in a black robe. Surrounding him were several men, broad-shouldered, brutish figures with hard, unforgiving faces. Each carried weapons—clubs, maces—hanging from their belts or resting on their shoulders.

Andreas narrowed his eyes. These men weren't vampires. Allies of the vampires, perhaps? Enforcers serving their vampiric masters in exchange for safety, power, or even immortality?

Perhaps they were coerced, compelled to serve under the threat of death. Vampires were creatures of the night, unable to walk freely in sunlight. They would need mortal agents to act on their behalf during the day.

"The vampires will kill us!" a villager cried out. "They've already started!"

The man in the black robe, clearly some kind of acolyte, raised a hand to quiet the murmurs spreading through the crowd. He was older than the others flanking him, his face deeply lined with wrinkles and his gray beard long and unkempt. His eyes gleamed with the kind of dangerous zeal that turned men into blind followers.

"Because of your hardness of heart, you were punished!" the acolyte bellowed. "But Valen, in his infinite mercy, seeks to bring you into his fold. Do you not desire to live forever with your loved ones? Then surrender your life to Valen!"

Eternal life. It echoed the very words that Jesus Christ had offered to His followers. But this was different. There was no Paradise in vampirism, only a twisted mockery of life. It wasn't eternity in the presence of God; it was an eternity of un-life. Not life forever, but death forever. A corpse forever. A hunger for blood that would never cease.

"And if we refuse?" another villager asked.

The acolyte gave a dark look. "Then even greater evil will befall your village."

The crowd exchanged nervous glances, their fear palpable.

"What must we do?" someone finally asked.

The acolyte smiled broadly, though the expression lacked any mirth. "Give your young to his majesty Valen."

"You ask for blood!" an outraged villager shouted.

"Yes, I do," the acolyte admitted without hesitation. "Blood is the stuff of life. It courses through our veins. It is a gift, an untapped resource of power that only Valen can awaken in all of us."

"You're mad!" someone yelled.

"I've had enough of this!" shouted another villager, his courage breaking through the fear. A handful of others echoed the sentiment. Slowly, a few of the villagers began to turn and leave.

Scowling, the acolyte pointed a bony finger at the retreating villagers. “Do not turn your back on Valen!”

At his signal, the men accompanying him unsheathed their clubs and advanced on the deserters.

“Oh, what have I done?” Decimus’s lament echoed in Andreas’s mind.

What had *Decimus* done? This wasn’t his fault.

Then a villager shouted, “I want eternal life!”

The dam broke. Others joined the desperate chorus.

“Me too!”

“Take my son! Make him a vampire!”

The acolyte spread his arms as though bestowing a blessing. “Then come! Tonight, you will live until the end of time itself!” His voice rang out like a twisted hymn. “Give your blood to Valen, and he shall grant you all that you desire!”

The frenzy escalated as the acolyte’s henchmen reached the fleeing villagers. They swung their clubs with brutal force. Cries of pain and terror tore through the air as the helpless were beaten down.

Andreas gripped the hilt of his black sword, his lahat chereb.

Then a quiet voice pierced through the bedlam.

"Wait."

Andreas turned to see a boy, perhaps no older than fourteen, draped in a tattered cloak with its hood pulled low over his face.

"You're the demon slayer, Andreas, aren't you?" the boy asked.

Andreas gave a curt nod. "What do you want?"

The boy glanced at the scene unfolding in the agora before turning back to Andreas. "You have to come with me. There's someone you must see. The villagers will suffer a few bruises, but they'll be safe. For now, at least. Valen and his vampires won't come out in daylight."

"Andreas," Decimus's voice spoke in his mind. *"Go with him. He'll lead you to one of the faithful, one of my flock. She's the one who summoned for you."*

Andreas studied the boy for a moment longer, then nodded again. "Lead the way."

VII

Andreas followed the boy to a modest house nestled at the edge of the village. It was unassuming: a single-story structure built from wood and mudbrick, its thatched roof sagging slightly with age.

Inside, the house was sparsely furnished. An unlit hearth occupied the far wall. Near the hearth sat a young woman, her back turned to them, her posture weary and hunched.

"I brought him, cousin," the boy said.

The young woman turned, and Andreas took her in. She was wrapped in a simple shawl with frayed edges draped over thin shoulders. Her green eyes held an innocent yet haunted quality, shining with a mixture of hope and trepidation. Her blond hair was tied back in a loose braid and the hollows beneath her eyes spoke of sleepless nights. Yet despite her obvious fatigue, she offered Andreas a warm smile.

"You must be Andreas, the demon slayer," she said, bowing her head. She couldn't have been more than fifteen or sixteen. And yet, something in her demeanor carried the weight of someone much older.

"Thank God, she lives," Decimus said. He recognized her. A member of his church, no doubt.

"My name is Marcia," she said. "And I'm the one who summoned for you."

Marcia gestured toward a small wooden table and offered him a seat. She fetched a loaf of bread from the counter, broke off a piece, and handed it to him. "Please, eat."

Andreas took the bread and sat, his black cloak shifting heavily around him as he lowered himself into the chair. The bread was somewhat stale, but he ate it without complaint. The boy who had led him here slipped out quietly, leaving them.

"Tell me," Andreas said, "what has happened in this village? Who are those men outside, preaching repentance through becoming vampires?"

"They call themselves the Blood Militia and follow Valen," Marcia said. "But they're still mortal. Valen employs them to keep the villagers in line during the day when he and his kind cannot walk under the sun. They're nothing more than brutes and savages."

"Are they from the village?"

She shook her head. "No. They hail from elsewhere, but I don't know where exactly." She paused, her gaze dropping to her hands. Her voice softened as she added, "Is—" She faltered, her throat bobbing as she swallowed before continuing, "Is Decimus well?"

"As well as he can be," Andreas replied. "He is within me, possessing my body. It allows him to leave the temple without fear of the scavenger demons hunting for his soul."

Marcia's shoulders relaxed, though the tension didn't fully leave her. "He came to see me once. After he...after he became a ghost. But the demons came for him, and he had to flee back to the temple. It was because he came to me that I summoned for you." Her fingers traced invisible patterns on the tabletop. "I wish I could see him again. I'm glad he's well, though."

"She is a sweet child," Decimus said, and Andreas could feel the warmth in the priest's words.

The Deathchaser harrumphed. *"She's quite the looker, I must say."*

"Are your carnal desires all you care about?"

"I am a demon, after all. Carnality is in my very being."

Enough, both of you! Andreas scolded inwardly. The Deathchaser's interruptions were tiresome on their own; adding Decimus to the mix made Andreas's head pound as if caught between clashing cymbals.

Focusing again on Marcia, Andreas asked, "And who are you, Marcia?"

She rose from her seat and crossed the room to the small window. The golden light of the setting sun bathed her in a warm glow. Outside, the sky was beginning to streak with purples and oranges, the day waning into night. Once the sun dipped below the horizon and the moon rose, how long until Valen and his vampires descended upon the village?

"I'm a follower of Christ," she said. "And I was a friend to Decimus's daughter, Cassia. At least, I thought I was."

Andreas frowned. "You thought?"

"Cassia had always been a high-spirited girl. She was bold, vibrant, and full of energy. I could barely keep up with her at times. She seemed to love life in a way I couldn't understand. She didn't just want to live—she wanted to be thrilled by everything. She sought out excitement like a moth to a flame." Her expression darkened. "But there was always something...restless about her, as if she were never satisfied, never content." She paused, then said, "I don't think I'm explaining this very well."

Seeking excitement for its own sake was far from the teachings of Christ. A true Christian was called to humility, selflessness, and simplicity. The joy of the faith came not from worldly thrills, but from prayer, fasting, and acts of charity.

"Sounds like my kind of girl," Andras remarked with a sly chuckle.

Andreas grimaced. *Is this true, Decimus?*

"I...I suppose so, yes."

It sounded as though Decimus was only now coming to terms with the true nature of his daughter's fiery, impulsive temperament. Surely, she must have shown signs of it before. Had he chosen to ignore them? Or perhaps she had worn a mask of humility and devotion in his presence, playing the part of the obedient, God-fearing daughter. Or worse still, had Decimus rationalized her behavior in his own mind, excusing it as a passing phase or harmless misstep?

"She used to pray with me," Marcia said. "Every day, faithfully. But then...she just stopped. It was so sudden, and I didn't know why. After that, everything began to change. It all started when Father Decimus found Valen."

"I should have left him to die," Decimus growled bitterly. *"If I had, none of this would have happened."*

"Oh my, priest!" Andras said gleefully. *"You sound just like me!"*

Andreas ignored the Deathchaser's mocking tone, though he made a mental note of Decimus's uncharacteristic outburst—a sentiment that was hardly becoming of a man of God.

"At first," Marcia continued, "Valen was so devout—more so than anyone else in the village, except for Father Decimus, of course. He prayed, he worked hard, and he helped wherever he could. But then, he changed, too. Slowly, he started pulling away from the faith. He and Cassia fell in love, but I don't think it was love. I think they were lost in lust." She blushed. "Please forgive me for speaking so bluntly."

For Andreas, there was little that could shock or offend him. Whatever Marcia had to share, he would hear it without judgment.

"It's all right," he said. "Do you know how Valen became a vampire?"

Marcia shook her head. "Two weeks ago, Decimus gathered all his followers—me, Cassia, everyone—and brought us to the temple. He said Valen had become a vampire and that he was coming for Cassia. He told us we could stop him with prayer if we worked together."

Andras grunted. *"A weak faith it must have been."*

"Could that have been true?" Decimus said. *"Was my faith truly so weak?"*

"Valen came for us," Marcia said, hugging herself. "It was like a nightmare. He..." She hesitated, the memory clearly a painful one. "He killed Father Decimus in front of us. Then he took Cassia. But it didn't stop there. He turned Fabian, Dosia, and Agrippa. Made them like him. Vampires."

"But you escaped? How?"

Marcia nodded. "Just barely. Agrippa tried to fight him. He was so brave. But I...I ran. I was terrified. I left them behind."

Her voice was strained. She shivered.

Outside, the sun dipped below the horizon, surrendering the sky to the creeping darkness of night.

"Your action was justified," Andreas said, rising from his seat. "Because you escaped, you were able to summon for me. That alone may save this village."

Marcia searched his face for reassurance. "Can you stop him? Can you save us—and Cassia?"

Andreas placed a hand on the hilt of his sword. "I will do all that I can."

Her shoulders slumped as she sighed heavily. A single tear traced a path down her cheek. "Thank you," she whispered.

"So, four vampires," the Deathchaser said. *"Perhaps five, if Valen turned Cassia—which he more than likely did."*

"But she can be changed back. You said so yourself. Slay Valen, and everyone he's turned will return to normal."

"There's a chance that might work," Andras conceded. *"There's also a chance it won't."*

"It has to!" Decimus's shout made Andreas flinch ever so slightly.

"Don't look at me, my dear Decimus. I don't make vampires or fiends. I only kill them—when it suits me."

Andreas sighed. The sooner this business was finished, the better. He turned his attention back to Marcia. "Do you know where Valen is hiding?"

"I'm afraid not. But the vampires come here at night." She glanced around nervously, then leaned in closer, her voice dropping to a whisper. "To feed."

A sudden knocking came at the door. Marcia yelped, her eyes widening. She gripped Andreas's arm.

"Open this door immediately!" a gruff voice demanded from the other side. "We know the demon slayer is with you, heathen!"

VIII

“The Blood Militia!” The blood drained from Marcia’s face. “They’ve come for us!”

Andreas gently gripped her shoulders, steadying her. “I’ll handle them,” he said. “They’re looking for me, not you. Find somewhere to hide.”

She nodded, but before she left, she gave him a simple wooden cross that she wore around her neck. “May God protect you.”

Andreas accepted the cross, his own pressing against his chest as it hung around his neck, tucked behind his leather armor. Though he had no need for a second cross, he tucked Marcia’s into the small pouch at his belt nonetheless.

Then Marcia disappeared into another room of the house. The faint sounds of furniture being shifted told Andreas she had found a hiding spot, likely concealed by the deep shadows of nightfall.

The banging on the door resumed, each impact sending shudders through the wooden frame.

Andreas undid the lock on the door and pulled it open. Standing before him was the elderly acolyte he had seen in the village agora. Behind him stood several of his henchmen, their clubs resting against their shoulders.

"You are the demon slayer?" the acolyte rasped, saliva dripping into his beard.

Andreas tapped the pommel of his black sword, the blade's unmistakable symbol of a demon slayer. "I am Andreas of Mount Athos."

The acolyte narrowed his sunken eyes. "You intend to slay my lord Valen?"

"Vampires are fiends of demons," Andreas said. "I cannot let him continue tormenting this village."

The night pressed down around them. An owl hooted somewhere in the distance, a dog barked sharply, and the buzz of cicadas filled the air.

"Come with us," the acolyte said. "Lord Agrippa and Lady Dosia wish to see you."

"Where is Valen?"

The acolyte grinned, revealing yellowed teeth. "Follow me," he said, stepping back to make way. "If you wish to know."

Andreas allowed himself to be escorted. The arrangement kept the Blood Militia distracted and, more importantly, away from Marcia. If they discovered she had summoned him, they wouldn't hesitate to kill her. Or worse. Flanked on both sides by the henchmen, Andreas walked without resistance.

As they moved through the village, doors creaked shut, and wooden shutters slammed into place. Villagers still outside scurried away, giving the acolyte and his men a wide berth.

"This must mean Valen turned Agrippa and Dosia," Decimus said. *"They were engaged to be married and faithful members of my church."*

Their path veered toward the village outskirts. Ahead, the Blood Militia was forcing villagers—men, women, and even children—into a large caged cart, one typically used to transport livestock.

Because that was all the villagers were to Valen—livestock.

"No!" A woman's anguished cry rang out as she ran toward the cart, tears streaming down her face. "Please! My son! Don't take my son from me!"

She dashed past two cloaked figures standing near the cart, their backs turned. Andreas's sharp eyes focused on them, catching a faint movement that was almost too fast to see.

Then it happened.

One of the figures moved—a blur of savage speed—and thrust a sword clean through the woman's throat.

Blood splattered on the grass below. The figure wrenched the blade free with brutal force, severing part of her neck. Her head dangled to one side, held by sinew and skin.

The woman crumpled to the ground with a dull, sickening thud.

A boy in the cart screamed. "Mama!"

The cloaked figures turned to face Andreas.

There was no mistaking it—they were vampires.

***

Horrified, Decimus watched through the portal in the black meadow as the gruesome scene unfolded. The mother's brutal murder left him speechless.

Her killer was Dosia—the sweet, soft-spoken woman he had once guided in faith. But this was not the Dosia he had known. This was a vampire wearing Dosia's face. Her pale skin gleamed like frost under moonlight, her eyes a chilling blend of gold and black, and her blood-red lips glistened as she brought her blade to her mouth, licking it clean of the woman's blood.

Decimus shivered, repulsed.

Beside him, the Deathchaser grunted and shook his head as if unimpressed by Dosia's theatrics.

Andreas stood still, his hand on the pommel of his black sword.

Next to Dosia was Agrippa. He, too, had undergone the horrific transformation into a vampire. His once modest frame now appeared broader and more imposing, his pale skin a ghastly white under the starlit sky. Fangs gleamed in his mouth.

Though their appearances still bore the semblance of the people Decimus once knew, it was clear their souls had been blackened. They were strangers now, nothing more than twisted echoes of their former selves.

"I brought him, my masters," the acolyte announced, bowing low in deference to the two vampires.

"Ah, so this is the demon slayer," Agrippa said, his voice unfamiliar. He looked at Andreas from top to bottom, and a corner of his mouth curved upwards in a crooked smile. "Impressive."

"He's quite handsome," Dosia purred. "Quite handsome, indeed." She ran her tongue across her lips. "I wager his blood tastes delicious."

"Perhaps Valen will allow us to keep him for ourselves," Agrippa said. "An eternity of fun."

"Release the villagers," Andreas said, his tone lacking any emotion.

The villagers, huddled together in the caged cart, had been led to believe they would be granted eternal life as vampires. But their grim reality was clear: they were nothing more than food. The cage was a macabre display of their fate, packed tightly like cattle destined for slaughter.

Agrippa crossed his muscular arms over his chest. "Demanding, are we not? These villagers belong to Valen, the Blood Prince. Their lives are his to command. He will do with them as he wills, and no one—certainly not you—can come between him and his desires."

"Who made Valen a vampire?" Andreas asked. "Do you know?"

Agrippa made a show of glancing at the night sky. "The night itself made him."

"They're toying with you, my boy," Andras muttered. Decimus could feel the demon's eagerness for violence.

Dosia let out a theatrical sigh, inspecting the dagger-like nails of her right hand. "I grow bored of this." She gave a dismissive wave of her pale hand. "Men, deal with him. But do not kill him. I want him alive."

The acolyte stepped aside as six henchmen encircled Andreas. Clubs thudded against their palms, and their voices rose in a cacophony of jeers and threats. Andreas, however, stood stock still.

To Decimus's astonishment, Andreas released his grip on the hilt of his black sword, letting it remain sheathed at his side.

Two of the henchmen charged, one lunging at Andreas from behind and another from his left. Decimus nearly cried out to warn him, but the Deatchchaser raised a hand, his tone calm but insistent.

"Watch," the demon said.

And so Decimus watched.

Andreas sidestepped one attacker, then threw a powerful punch at the first henchman, and a swift kick to the ribs disabled the second. When a third swung his club, Andreas ducked, grabbed the man by his waist, and tossed him over his shoulder as if he weighed nothing.

The final three men charged in desperation. Andreas met them head-on. His strikes were calculated, each blow landing with devastating force. In seconds, the last henchman crumpled to the ground, groaning in pain alongside his defeated comrades.

Decimus's mouth hung open in shock.

"Look at him," the Deathchaser said with pride. "Magnificent, isn't he?"

"Oh, my! That was delightful!" Dosia cooed. She shamelessly touched herself, her fingers grazing between her legs, then moving to squeeze her blood-streaked breasts. A disturbing, twisted smile spread across her face, the fight clearly arousing her.

"What has become of you, Dosia?" Decimus whispered. He could barely stand to watch her, his heart sinking into a pit of despair.

Agrippa licked his lips. "You've proven yourself a worthy adversary, demon slayer," he said. "And now, I want you even more."

Andreas drew his black sword. A flicker of blue fire ignited along the weapon's edge.

"I've no time for your games," Andreas said, his voice cold.

Decimus shuddered as he felt the power of the blade stir within Andreas. The energy was extraordinary—a tempest ready to be unleashed. A beautiful, righteous power that was all within the sword. This was aether, the power of angels and demons.

Andras whispered a curse. The demon, usually smug and confident, seemed shaken. His hands squeezed into white-knuckled fists.

The holy power of the blade—it was affecting him.

Was the sword's sanctified aether burning Andras within Andreas's body? And if it was harming the demon, what did that mean for Andreas?

He felt it, too—a fire burning within the demon slayer, threatening to consume him entirely. The pain reverberated through Decimus, and he could only imagine the torment Andreas himself endured.

"What a magnificent sword!" Dosia said.

Agrippa smirked. "It shall make a fine trophy for Prince Valen. A token of our—"

Before Agrippa could finish, Andreas exploded into motion, a burst of pure aether propelling him forward with terrifying speed at the vampire couple.

Andreas raised his flaming sword and brought it down with devastating force. The black blade should have cleaved through Agrippa.

But it didn't.

Instead, the blade collided with a barrier of blood: a glistening, crimson wall that enveloped the vampire couple. The flames hissed and the sword bit into the barrier, but it did not pierce it. The unholy shield absorbed the impact, sending ripples through its viscous surface before repelling the blade entirely.

Agrippa smiled savagely. "Oops," he said before his foot lashed out with unnatural speed, connecting with Andreas's chest and sending him staggering backward.

The vampire couple drew their own blades, their movements synchronized. The blood shield surrounding them collapsed with a grisly slurping sound.

In perfect unison, Agrippa and Dosia lunged toward Andreas. Their attacks came swiftly, a chaotic storm of steel and feral energy. Andreas met each blow with a deft parry, his blade ringing out with sharp, metallic clashes. But their speed was overwhelming; one strike flowed seamlessly into the next, leaving him no room to counterattack.

Their laughter was sharp and grating: Dosia's high-pitched cackle mingling with Agrippa's guttural chuckles.

Decimus, watching through the portal in Andreas's mind, felt their power surge around them like a fog. It was vile; it corrupted, drained, and filled the air with an icy menace.

The Deathchaser, who had been observing silently, stood abruptly in the black meadow. He glared at the vampire couple. A gust of wind swept through the meadow. Overhead, thunder cracked in the mind of Andreas.

The dark power shifted. It no longer emanated solely from the vampires. Now, it coursed through Andreas, and its source was Andras. The Deathchaser's malevolence surged with an intensity that dwarfed the combined aether of Agrippa and Dosia.

Andreas lunged forward, aiming for Agrippa, but as his blade descended, the blood shield reappeared instantaneously. The black sword collided with it, its fiery edge hissing as it failed to penetrate the barrier.

"Split them apart, my boy!" Andras roared.

Clearly, the blood shield was some kind of vampiric sorcery, and one that repelled even the blade of a holy sword. Was its power tied to Agrippa and Dosia's proximity to one another? They hadn't attempted to flank Andreas, staying close as if their connection was essential.

Andreas leapt backward, his boots crunching against the dirt, creating much-needed space between him and the vampire couple. Both hands gripped the hilt of the black sword. The flames along the blade intensified, their blue hue darkening.

Decimus cried out in Andreas's mind. "The flames! They're burning me!"

"Oh, quit your whining, priest!" the Deathchaser snapped.

Andreas swung the sword in a wide arc, though he was still several paces from his opponents. It wasn't the blade that mattered—it was the fire. The flames roared from the sword like a tidal wave, a deafening crackle that seemed to consume the very air around it. The heat of the attack scorched the ground, leaving trails of smoldering ash in its wake.

Decimus was stunned. There was no way that the blood shield, impressive as it was, could withstand such hallowed power.

It seemed Agrippa and Dosia reached the same conclusion. Their predatory confidence shattered as their golden eyes widened in panic. They leapt in opposite directions, the fiery inferno roaring past where they had stood.

Separated.

Andreas's eyes narrowed. It was the opportunity he had been waiting for. He charged toward Agrippa, the black sword blazing in his hands. The vampire staggered as Andreas closed in, raising his blade defensively.

The first strike was swift but shallow, the edge of the black sword grazing Agrippa's cheek. The vampire hissed in pain as dark blood welled from the wound. He tried to retreat, but his foot caught on uneven ground. Agrippa slipped, losing his balance, and fell backward with a grunt, landing hard on the earth.

"Husband!" Dosia's voice rang out as she scrambled to rejoin him.

Andreas raised his sword high, prepared to drive it through Agrippa's throat.

"Don't!"

The cry was desperate. Andreas froze mid-strike, the point of his sword hovering mere inches above Agrippa's neck.

It was Marcia, her hands clasped tightly against her chest. "You can save them, can't you? Don't kill them!"

Hope flared in Decimus. If Valen were slain, Agrippa and Dosia might return to who they once were. Marcia knew that, and her desperate words were a timely reminder for the demon slayer.

Andreas pulled the weapon back and retreated a few steps.

In the black meadow, the Deathchaser let out a long, exasperated groan. "You foolish mortals. Always so hopeful. Always so weak."

Dosia darted forward, crouching beside her husband. Agrippa sat up, blood seeping from the shallow cut on his cheek. She leaned in close to him, her eyes glowing with hunger. With a serpentine movement, she licked the trail of blood from his wound.

A deep, shuddering sigh escaped her lips, her mouth now painted crimson with Agrippa's blood. A feral energy crackled between them. Agrippa growled low in his throat, his eyes burning with primal intensity.

He grabbed Dosia's hair, yanking her head back. She gasped; not in pain, but in exhilaration. He dug his fangs into the pale flesh of her neck.

And he began to feed.

Dosia moaned with pleasure.

"They're..." Decimus could not believe his eyes. "They're feeding on each other!"

IX

Blood trickled from their mouths. Dosia flashed her fangs and sank them deep into the nape of Agrippa's neck as Decimus continued to watch from the black meadow.

As she fed on him, Agrippa grinned. "Dosia and I share a unique ability among vampires. When we drink each other's blood, our aether grows stronger. We become drunk with each other's essence and fall into a frenzy."

Dosia pulled away with a satisfied sigh. She licked her lips, savoring the taste. "A blood frenzy."

The force of their aether rose like a storm about to break.

"How?" Decimus whimpered within Andreas's mind. "How can one man hope to defeat them?"

Next to him, Andras cursed. "Here they come!" he said. "Quick, my boy! Use me!"

Andreas did, pulling on the dark aether of the Deathchaser. Within the black meadow, the petals of the ebony flowers stirred in a mighty wind. They lifted into the air, spiraling in chaotic gusts.

The vampires attacked, their movements a blur, their swords flashing like lightning. Each strike they delivered was more ferocious than the last, their strength amplified by their blood frenzy.

Andreas blocked and parried their blows with his black sword. The clang of steel on steel echoed like thunder, each impact shaking the air. In the black meadow of Andreas's mind, the storm raged more violently. Lightning cracked the skies above. Thunder rolled in waves.

Andreas's endurance astonished Decimus. Strike after strike, blow after blow, the demon slayer held his ground. But it was clear he was tiring. Sweat dripped down his face. His breaths came heavier, his movements fractionally slower. He couldn't keep this pace forever.

In the black meadow, the storm reached a crescendo. A bolt of lightning struck the ground in front of

Decimus, sending a shock wave rippling outward. Though he was no longer alive, a chilling fear gripped him. Could even a spirit feel pain here in this realm of the mind and soul?

Dosia's blade flashed out, faster than Andreas could react. The edge sliced cleanly across his shoulder. He stumbled back, clutching the wound as blood seeped through his fingers and stained his cloak. His chest rose and fell with labored breaths.

Dosia lifted her sword, Andreas's blood glistening on the blade, and brought it to her lips. She licked the blade clean.

"I was right," she purred. "Very tasty, indeed."

The vampires closed in once more. Agrippa lunged at Andreas from the right, while Dosia came at him from the left. Their strikes were relentless, forcing Andreas back on the defensive. He deflected one attack, only for another to come an instant later.

"Something's wrong," Andras said, his arms crossed over his chest. His normally glib demeanor was replaced by a grim expression. Around them, the storm raged, the wind howling and petals swirling in the black meadow.

"What do you mean?" Decimus asked. The demon's sudden seriousness unsettled him even more than his usual sarcasm.

"Even with their blood frenzy, their aether is still no match for what Andreas is capable of. I can tell that much."

"Then what's happening?"

The Deathchaser glared at him. Decimus recoiled.

"You," Andras growled, his words striking like a hammer. "You are doing this. Your presence inside Andreas is siphoning his aether."

"But...but what if I left his body?"

No.

It was Andreas. Even amidst the chaos of battle, his focus encompassed everything—his enemies, his demon, and Decimus within him.

If you do that, Andreas continued, *the scavenger demons will come in droves. I cannot fight both these vampires and those demons. The villagers will suffer.*

The Deathchaser swore, then said, "You're going to get killed if you don't think of something! Just do away with them! Kill them, my boy, and save yourself!"

"No, please!" Decimus begged. "If there is even a chance to save them—"

I will not kill them, Andreas confirmed.

The Deathchaser scowled at Decimus.

Again, Andreas broke from the engagement, retreating to put some distance between himself and the vampires. He stood hunched over, the point of his sword touching the grass beneath him. The weapon was not only a tool of destruction but also a double-edged burden, draining him with every passing moment it remained ignited.

I have an idea. Though I'm not sure if it will work.

Andras grunted. "A risk, then? Lovely. Just what we need."

"Give it up, demon slayer," Agrippa said. Unlike Andreas, neither Agrippa nor Dosia showed any sign of fatigue. They stood tall, their bodies thrumming with the aether of their blood frenzy.

"He is truly something, isn't he?" Dosia remarked. "Tell me, are all demon slayers like you?"

Andras smirked darkly. "She has no idea."

Agrippa raised his sword, pointing the tip of the blade at Andreas. "I'm going to enjoy sucking every last drop of your blood."

As one, they went after Andreas, who responded in kind, channeling a surge of aether through his body and mind. Agrippa struck first. Andreas savagely deflected the blow, the force of his counter sending Agrippa staggering backward. Without hesitation, Andreas dropped his sword and spun around to face Dosia, who was already bringing her weapon down upon him.

Andreas stepped into her attack, leaning his weight against her. His left hand shot out, gripping the hilt of her sword, stopping it mid-strike. Dosia's golden eyes widened in fury and surprise, but before she could react further, Andreas reached into his pouch with his free hand and pulled out the wooden cross he had taken from Marcia.

He planted the cross firmly against Dosia's chest.

A bloodcurdling scream tore from the vampire's throat as the holy artifact seared through her armor and into her pale flesh. Smoke rose in thick, acrid tendrils, carrying with it the sickening stench of charred, rotting meat. Dosia's body convulsed as the cross burned deeper into her, its divine power overwhelming her dark aether.

Andreas swept his leg out, tripping Dosia and sending her sprawling onto the ground. Her back hit the dirt with a heavy thud, and still, she screamed, clawing feebly at the cross as it pulsed with radiant energy, pinning her to the earth like an immovable weight.

Andreas stood over her, his chest heaving from the exertion. The cross remained embedded in Dosia's chest, its holiness radiating like a small sun. She writhed beneath its force, her screams filling the night air, but she could not remove it; could not escape its purifying light.

"Dosia!" Agrippa shouted.

"Don't move," Andreas commanded. He bent down, retrieving his sword from the ground. Its blue flames had extinguished. Andreas placed the edge beneath Dosia's chin, the steel biting into her pale flesh. "Move an inch, and I'll cut her throat."

Andreas's threat was calculated, but Decimus prayed it was only a bluff.

The threat worked. Agrippa froze in place, his once-arrogant demeanor crumbling into one of submission. The grip on his sword loosened.

"Don't hurt her!" Agrippa pleaded. "Please!"

"I wasn't sure if this would work," Andreas admitted, smiling faintly. "When I saw the crosses and icons in the temple desecrated, I suspected Valen was behind it. Not all vampires are repelled by holy objects, but it seems you two didn't inherit your maker's immunity."

Agrippa glowered. "You bastard!"

"Throw your weapon," Andreas demanded.

"Don't, husband!" Dosia gasped. She had stopped screaming, but the cross still pressed against her chest rendered her utterly powerless. "Kill him now!"

In response, Andreas pressed the blade closer to her throat, the edge biting just enough to draw a thin line of blood.

"What are you going to do, Agrippa?" Andreas asked. "Make your decision. Quickly."

Agrippa looked between his sword, his immobilized wife, and Andreas's unwavering stance. After a tense moment, he tossed his sword aside.

"Good," Andreas said. He withdrew his sword from Dosia's neck and stood upright. "You stay right there."

Dosia writhed. She hissed through gritted teeth. "You'll pay for this, slayer," she spat, her voice a raspy growl.

Andreas ignored her threats and strode to Agrippa. The vampire did not move, only continued to glower.

"What now?" Agrippa said. "Will you slay me here and now?"

Andreas smiled. "Not quite. I've a better idea." He reached into his leather armor, pulling free a leather cord from which hung a small silver cross.

Agrippa's eyes widened in realization, and he instinctively stepped back.

But it was too late—Andreas pressed the cross against Agrippa's neck.

The vampire let out an earsplitting howl as the cross burned into his flesh. Smoke curled from the point of contact, and Agrippa fell to his knees. His agony mirrored Dosia's; paralyzing, consuming, absolute.

"Quickly, Marcia!" Andreas called over his shoulder. "Free the villagers while they're incapacitated. We'll put these two in the cage!"

X

Marcia freed the villagers from the cage. The villagers were grateful as they stumbled out into the open air. Using the divine power of the cross, Andreas compelled Agrippa and Dosia into the now-vacated cage. The vampires, still paralyzed by the crosses, hissed and snarled in defiance but could do little else.

Before removing the crosses, Andreas gave clear instructions to Marcia. "Bring garlic. As much as you can find."

Marcia relayed the order, and soon villagers returned with bundles of garlic bulbs. Andreas directed them to place the garlic in the cage with the vampires and to surround the stable, where they had moved the cage to, with the pungent plant.

"Garlic has long been a symbol of purity and protection," Andreas explained. "Much like the cross of Christ, it repels vampires and dulls their abilities."

Satisfied with the preparations, Andreas inspected the cage one final time. The vampires were subdued, their furious glares and venomous curses losing potency behind the barrier of garlic and holy power.

"The stable roof will protect them from sunlight until I slay Valen," Andreas said. "When that is done, we will see them restored."

The Blood Militia received a different fate. Bound tightly with rope, their arms and legs immobilized, they were imprisoned in another corner of the stable. The cage was large enough to fit them alongside the vampires, but Andreas knew better.

By the time the work was done, the night was deep, and the stars shone coldly overhead. The air felt heavy with tension, but the adrenaline coursing through Marcia's veins kept her alert. She sat beside Andreas in the stable, gazing at the caged vampires.

Agrippa and Dosia. They were barely recognizable now. Marcia's memories of them flashed vividly in her mind: Agrippa's quiet strength, Dosia's warm smile. They had been like siblings to her, family through faith. She had rejoiced at the announcement of their engagement, looking forward to celebrating their union. Now, that future seemed so far away, so unlikely.

"Tell me of Cassia," Andreas demanded of the vampires. "Is she still of man?"

"She is still alive," Agrippa said, his words slightly slurred. He sat cross-legged, his back slumped against the iron bars of the cage.

"That did not answer my question."

Marcia shivered at his tone. Despite being on the same side, she found Andreas almost as unsettling as the vampires themselves. He had an abrasiveness to him that seemed unbecoming of a follower of Jesus. Then again, only those anointed by the Lord could wield the powers of a demon slayer—or so she thought.

"We don't know what's become of her," Dosia answered. She lay on her side, her head resting in Agrippa's lap. "Valen keeps her to himself. We haven't seen her since the night at the temple."

"Is it possible she escaped Valen?"

"Highly unlikely," Agrippa said, absently stroking Dosia's hair. "Valen is possessive. He wants her all to himself."

The Valen Marcia remembered had been nothing like this creature they spoke of. He had been gentle and kind, even humble. Could his lust for Cassia have twisted him so completely?

No—it was more likely Cassia had changed him.

"She may still be of man," Dosia said. "But if she is, she has likely been drained of her blood to the very inch of her life. I have no doubt Valen feeds on her daily."

"Where is Valen?" Andreas asked.

Silence from the vampires. Their mouths clamped shut, their gazes darting anywhere but toward him.

"Please, Agrippa, Dosia," Marcia urged. "Don't you remember the times we had together? We prayed together. We took communion together. We were baptized together."

Dosia shot her a dark look. "I always despised you. You were like a lapdog to Decimus. He would say, 'Jump,' and you would ask, 'How high?'" She spat. "You disgust me."

"You should be one of us," Agrippa said. "The priest is dead. Your faith can't save you."

Their words were like acid, corroding her resolve. She had never been strong, always doing what others wanted of her, bending to their will like a reed in the wind. But choosing Christ had been her first true decision, her own act of will. It was the right decision, too; she believed that with all her heart. She held fast to the promise of Jesus, for blessed are the meek, for they shall inherit the earth.

"But perhaps my faith can save you," Marcia said, humbly. "I will pray for you. Both of you."

Agrippa snorted derisively. "Save your breath."

"Enough," Andreas said. He placed a hand on Marcia's shoulder. She looked away, blushing. Despite his gruff demeanor, there was something striking about him. His strength, his confidence, his sheer presence.

Andreas turned his steely gaze back to the caged vampires. "I'll ask again—where is Valen?"

"Do you take us for fools?" Dosia said.

"And don't think of asking the Blood Militia," Agrippa added. "They know nothing of Valen's whereabouts. They have only encountered Valen once and mainly deal with us."

"What does Valen want?" Andreas asked.

Agrippa shrugged. "Blood, of course."

"Is that all? Food? What does he want with the villagers?"

"None of your damned business, demon slayer."

Or they didn't know. Whatever Valen was planning, perhaps he hadn't shared it with his fledglings. Still, it was hard to believe Valen's ambitions ended with Cassia. If she were his only goal, why such a relentless focus on terrorizing the villagers?

If they didn't know Valen's full intentions, they at least knew his location. Andreas drew his cross necklace into the open.

"I will not ask again."

The vampires recoiled. Dosia hissed like a cornered animal, while Agrippa glared. It struck Marcia how strange it was that the cross of Christ—an emblem of salvation and grace—could be wielded as a weapon, a threat.

Strange, and saddening, too. Marcia's heart ached for Agrippa and Dosia. She had already wept for them after the events at the temple, but seeing them now, so consumed by darkness, she felt the sting of fresh tears welling in her eyes.

"Very well," Dosia acquiesced.

"Dosia!"

"I will not go through that torture again! It's bad enough we have to deal with this damned stinking garlic!" She gave Andreas a sharp look. "Besides, you'll never defeat Fabian."

Andreas seemed unperturbed. "Let me worry about that."

"There is a villa to the northwest of here along the coast of the Adriatic Sea."

"I know the place," Marcia said. "It's not far from here."

Andreas nodded. "Then I leave immediately. Leave them here. With the garlic, they can't escape the cage."

Marcia followed Andreas out of the stable. As they left, Agrippa shouted, "You will die! You will become food for the Blood Prince! Mark my words, demon slayer!"

Andreas shut the stable door behind them. The stable's owner, grateful for Andreas's intervention in saving his son from the vampires, had offered him a horse and saddle. The animal, a sturdy brown steed, was tethered to a nearby tree. Andreas climbed up and into the saddle while Marcia untied the horse.

"If I follow the coastline, will I reach the villa?" Andreas asked.

"Yes, you should. But why not rest? You're tired, and your wound—"

"I've been through worse," Andreas interrupted. "Besides, I won't engage Valen or Fabian at night. Most vampires sleep during the day."

Most? Did that mean there were vampires powerful enough to move freely in daylight, unaffected by the sun's purifying light?

"Please wait," Marcia said. "I have something for you."

Marcia hurried back to her modest home and gathered supplies for the demon slayer. She packed a loaf of bread, a skin of water, and as many crosses as she could find. Some of those crosses, she realized with a pang, Valen had carved himself.

Returning to Andreas, she handed him a small sack filled with the supplies.

"This should help you on your journey," she said.

Andreas bowed his head. "You are too kind. Thank you, Marcia."

"Please bring back Cassia. And Fabian, too."

"I will. Now get some rest."

He tugged at the reins and kicked the horse into a gallop. Marcia stood there, watching as Andreas disappeared into the distance.

Alone now, she clasped her hands together and mouthed a silent prayer.

Lord, keep him safe. And bring them all back to us.

XI

With the battle over, a strange serenity settled over the black meadow.

Decimus lowered himself to the ground, seated next to Andras. The two faced the view portal, showing Andreas riding his borrowed horse along the coastline.

Andras, meanwhile, entertained himself with the peculiar flora of the meadow. He had plucked one of the black flowers, its stem bending limply. He crushed the flower into a ball, and before Decimus's eyes, the crumpled petals transformed. Eight spindly black legs sprouted from the mass, forming a spider-like creature. Andras let it crawl leisurely between his fingers.

"Why did you choose Andreas?" Decimus asked, breaking the silence.

The demon tilted his head. "You wish to learn about your enemy, priest?"

"You are not my enemy, Andras."

"Not presently," Andras admitted, watching the spider-thing as it scuttled over his hand. "But let us not pretend, my dear Decimus. I am a demon. This form I wear may appear almost noble, but I loathe mankind. Every last one of you. Do you know what the demons of Hades call me?"

"What?" Decimus asked cautiously.

Andras crushed the spider in his palm. The creature crumbled into dust. Opening his hand, he blew the remains toward Decimus.

"They call me the Deathchaser," Andras said with dark pride. "Because I love to kill."

Decimus frowned. "Why are you avoiding my question?"

Andras laughed, a guttural, chilling sound. "Because, my dear Decimus, it's none of your damned business why I chose to possess Andreas."

"We have a while yet before we reach the villa," Decimus said. There was little he knew about Andreas or the demon inside him. The tales of Andreas of

Mount Athos had reached him during his travels across the Roman Empire. "You seem to care for Andreas."

"I am simply concerned for the body I possess."

"You're not fooling me, Andras. You could always possess another body. But it's Andreas you want. I could even say you love him. As a father might love his son."

That sparked something in Andras. Though Decimus was certain the Deathchaser wouldn't harm him in the black meadow, the dark look he gave him was full of ruin.

"Careful, priest," Andras growled. "Just because we are spending time together does not make us friends."

"I've noticed," Decimus pressed on, "that you often refer to him as 'my boy.' Why is that?"

Andras fully turned to face Decimus. He picked another flower, twirling it between his fingers. "I'll make a deal with you, priest. I'll answer one of your questions if you answer one of mine."

Decimus hesitated. This was the second time Andras had tried to pry into him.

He could not confide in Andras. That would be foolish. The Deathchaser was not a spiritual father, nor a confidant. He was a demon. To confess to him would be to risk everything.

And yet—part of Decimus wanted to. Unburdening himself, even to a demon, was oddly tempting. Would confessing bring the angels for his soul? Would it offer him a chance at redemption?

But no. Even if he confessed, could he repent?

The answer, Decimus realized bitterly, was no. He would not repent. He could not repent.

He would rather embrace Hades.

“Scared, are we?” Andras said.

Decimus sighed. “Very well. But I go first.”

“Fine with me.” Andras settled back with a casual air, though his scarlet eyes gleamed with mischief.

“Why Andreas?”

The demon rolled his eyes dramatically, as though the question bored him. “The boy possesses a power I have never seen before. And I’m not talking about what he can do with his lahat chereb or the darkness he borrows from me.” He paused, leaning closer, his voice dropping to an almost reverent tone. “He has an aether that is his own. Most demon slayers do, but Andreas’s power is exceptional. I want that power for myself.”

“Then why not possess Andreas entirely?”

Andras wagged a finger at him. “Ah, ah, ah, my turn, priest.” His expression darkened. “Do you love your daughter?”

Decimus blinked, his spine stiffening. “What kind of question is that?”

“An honest one that begs an honest answer,” Andras said. “Do you love your daughter?”

“Of course, I do.”

“More than yourself?” Andras pressed, his tone low.

Decimus frowned. “I don’t understand you.”

Andras waved a hand dismissively. “Nothing. Go on. Your turn.”

“You already know the question.”

The demon sighed, leaning back with exaggerated weariness. “Andreas’s aether protects him from my taking complete control over him. Though...there have been a handful of times where I was close. But he always finds a way to claw himself back from the depths of the black meadow.”

“This place,” Decimus said, gesturing to the dark, eerie landscape around them. “It’s your doing, then?”

Andras grunted. “I’ll answer this one for free. Yes, this place is my sanctuary. It was also Andreas’s sanctuary as a child when he was exposed to demonic rituals by his own mother and her freakish, demon-loving cult.”

The revelation chilled Decimus. Of all the rumors he'd heard about Andreas, none of them had hinted at this. "That's...ghastly."

"Don't worry," the Deathchaser said, his grin widening, fire flickering in his eyes. "I took care of them."

Decimus shuddered despite the relative warmth of the meadow.

"My turn—" Andras cleared his throat theatrically, then his eyes drilled into Decimus and he asked, "Why did you kill Valen?"

Decimus's stomach clenched; his throat bobbed; his mouth felt as dry as parchment.

Andras cocked his head, feigning concern. "What's the matter, my dear Decimus? Don't want to play anymore?"

"I..."

It was all he could manage.

And just as he felt he might fall into the abyss within himself, Andreas's voice echoed through the black meadow:

We've arrived.

The Deathchaser shrugged. "I have my answer," he muttered, turning towards the view portal.

XII

Mirko had been a devout follower of Absalona for as long as he could remember. Her worship was etched into his very being, as natural as the flow of blood in his veins. It was all he knew, all he had been taught. His family, long before his birth, had been steadfast in their devotion to the once-great blood goddess.

They weren't alone. Other families, scattered and diminished now, had also worshiped Absalona. They all traced their bloodlines back to the very first disciples of the blood: a proud and ancient lineage.

But then the Romans came.

The invaders slaughtered nearly all the faithful. Temples were burned, relics desecrated, and the sacred bloodletting rituals were extinguished under the crushing weight of Roman steel. Only a handful of disciples managed to escape, fleeing into the shadows like hunted animals.

Mirko hadn't even been born when the massacre occurred, but he knew the stories well. They had been passed down, one generation to the next, a grim and angry litany of loss and vengeance. Those tales were the heartbeat of his faith, his unshakable belief that the blood goddess would rise again and restore what had been stolen.

Yet as the years passed and the Roman grip tightened, there was no one left to openly worship Absalona. The village, once a stronghold of the blood goddess's power, was now home to those who knew nothing of her glory. The villagers went about their mundane lives, ignorant and indifferent to the goddess.

But they would know her again.

The blood goddess would rise once more, and Mirko was certain he would be the instrument of her vengeance. It was his purpose, his destiny. Rome would pay for its transgressions, and the village would once again tremble beneath the weight of Absalona's divine wrath.

Though Mirko could not help but wonder—

Why had Absalona chosen Valen as her vampire?

The Roman was a killer. A traitor. A man unworthy of the goddess's favor. It disgusted Mirko that such a man should become the vessel of Absalona's will.

Why not himself?

Mirko knelt in the villa that Valen and his vampires had seized as their own. The once-opulent residence, owned by a gluttonous merchant, now bore the stench of death and decay. Outside the villa's walls, the merchant's bloated corpse lay among the lifeless bodies of his servants, all of them drained of blood.

"A demon slayer has come, my prince," Mirko announced. He kept his head bowed. It took every ounce of restraint not to let his disdain show. To him, Valen was no prince, despite the title he had so arrogantly claimed. He was a vampire, yes, but in Mirko's eyes, he was nothing more than a tool for the blood goddess.

Valen reclined lazily in a grand chair that bore the air of a makeshift throne. A polished dark wood table stood before him, adorned with plates of rotting fruit, attracting flies and wasps.

"A demon slayer," Valen mused. "I remember tales of such warriors from my mortal days as a Roman soldier."

Mirko remained bowed. "He is no ordinary man, my prince. He defeated both Agrippa and Dosia."

Though those two were the weakest of the vampires Valen had made; hence why they were always together.

"They fought while you scurried away?" Valen's tone was as cold as the grave.

Bastard! Mirko seethed, though he masked his rage. Clearing his throat, he said, "Only to come and warn you, my prince."

Valen rose from his grand chair and sauntered over to Mirko, who remained kneeling. The vampire's shadow fell over him.

"So," Valen drawled, "not only do you come to me empty-handed, but you bring the news that my scions have been defeated and my Blood Militia decimated. This must be one truly impressive demon slayer."

The vampire prince didn't seem remotely concerned. Did he truly think himself invincible?

"He may thwart our plans," Mirko said.

Valen shot him an icy look. "*Our* plans?"

A fire burned in Mirko's stomach and the back of his throat felt raw. He forced himself to remain composed. "*Your* plans, my prince," he corrected. "I meant no offense. I live only to serve you, for you are the chosen one of Absalona."

A part of him longed to see this demon slayer plunge a sword through Valen's heart, ending the vampire's immortality. *But think of Absalona. Only of Absalona.*

"Indeed." Valen turned away from Mirko, his dark cloak sweeping the floor. "Thank you for your report, my dear Mirko." He returned to his chair and plopped down in it with a flourish, lounging as though he had not a single care in the world. "You may go. Return to the villagers and continue spreading the gospel of Absalona."

"As you wish, my prince."

Mirko rose and left the dining hall, and then the villa. He mounted his horse and started his way back to the village.

All the while hating the vampire he was forced to call prince.

***

With Mirko gone, the villa grew quiet. Valen remained seated in his grand chair, lounging with one leg draped over the armrest, appearing every bit the arrogant ruler he fancied himself to be. Yet he was not alone.

From the thick shadows in the corner of the room, Fabian emerged. The darkness clung to him like a second skin. It was his gift, this ability to blend seamlessly with shadows. But Valen had sensed his presence long before Fabian chose to reveal himself.

"Master," Fabian said. "We have a visitor."

Valen raised an eyebrow, feigning mild interest. "A visitor, you say?"

"A man in a black cloak and carrying a black sword."

"Ah," Valen said with a smirk. "The demon slayer Mirko so helpfully warned us about. It seems Agrippa and Dosia lacked the foresight to keep their mouths shut. No matter."

Fabian grimaced. "Marcia must have summoned for the demon slayer. We should not have let her live."

"An oversight," Valen agreed, his tone dismissive, "but a minor one."

Valen wasn't concerned, and why should he be? Since his rebirth, he possessed a power only few could dream of, and more than that, he was immortal.

Wasn't eternal life the cornerstone of Decimus's endless sermons? Hadn't the priest preached that Jesus alone was the path to immortality? How misguided he had been.

He was living proof that eternal life required no forgiveness, no prayer, no fasting, no penance. Who needed healing from sin when immortality flowed in your veins?

All Valen needed was blood. And there was plenty of it to go around.

"Perhaps this demon slayer slew Agrippa and Dosia," Fabian said.

"No. They are alive. I can still feel them." Valen chuckled. "It could be that the demon slayer believes he can save them and somehow return them to their mortality. Utter foolishness."

"I will kill him."

Fabian began to retreat into the shadows, but Valen raised a hand, staying him.

"No. Not yet. Let him be. We get so few visitors to our new home."

"You are too lenient, master."

Valen narrowed his gaze. "You question me?"

"N-no, master," Fabian was quick to say. "I merely voice my concerns."

"If you are so eager, then who am I to get in the way of that? Do with him as you will."

Fabian bowed his head. "Thank you, master."

"Now leave me."

Fabian nodded and melted back into the shadows of the dining hall, vanishing. The room grew still again.

Once Fabian was gone, Valen left the dining hall and navigated through the dimly lit corridors to a set of stairs that ascended to the second floor. At the top, he pushed open the door to a grand bedroom. The room was lavishly appointed, with velvet drapes covering the windows and a massive bed covered in black silks at its center.

There, sitting on a chair looking out of a balcony to the Adriatic Sea was his most precious possession.

Cassia, his bride. Her eyes were closed and her hands rested delicately in her lap. She appeared at peace.

Valen approached her.

"My love," he whispered, kneeling in front of her, taking her hands into his own. "A demon slayer has come to take you from me."

His words hung in the air, unanswered. Cassia remained still, silent.

Valen leaned closer. "But I won't let him. I swear it. I will protect you, always. I will keep you safe from anyone who dares to come between us."

He embraced her tenderly. He rested his head against hers, closing his eyes as though drawing strength from her stillness.

"Oh, how I love you," he murmured. "I could not be without you. Not even death could keep me from you."

Cassia stirred. Her eyelids fluttered open. Slowly, her lips curved into a gentle, knowing smile.

Valen exhaled in relief, his expression breaking into one of pure adoration. "You are my everything, Cassia," he said. "And I will ensure no one—no demon slayer, no god, no one—will ever take you from me."

Cassia's smile deepened, enigmatic yet affectionate, as though she understood far more than she let on. She raised a hand, trailing her fingers lightly across Valen's cheek. He leaned into her touch, his heart alight with the certainty that she was his, and his alone.

XIII

Weeping willows hid the villa from prying eyes and a morning mist clung to the villa's grim marble walls. Thorny vines and twisted ivy crawled up the columns like veins over the stone, their leaves a sickly green almost gray as though the residing darkness had sucked the life from them.

Above, there was not a cloud in the sky, the sun shining brightly and warmly. A blessed day—one that any vampire would surely detest.

Andreas had slept a few hours before dawn broke. Though he kept his black sword close to him, the night had passed without incident. He had his horse tethered to a nearby tree.

"Do vampires sleep during the day?" Decimus asked.

"Most do, yes," Andreas said. He stood atop a small hill, scanning the villa below for any sign of the enemy and finding none. If anything, the villa looked abandoned and neglected. "But some vampires can endure the sunlight, though it weakens their aether."

"But why is that?" Decimus pressed.

"Oh, come now, priest. Surely you must know. Light versus dark, good versus evil. Hasn't the sun always been a symbol of the Lord's wretched holiness and nauseating goodness?"

"Well, yes," Decimus said, nervously. *"I suppose so."*

"That isn't the only reason," Andreas said. "The sun's light is the source of life itself. It gives energy to plants, sustenance to animals, and vitality to us mortals. Its very existence represents growth and renewal, qualities that directly oppose the nature of vampires."

"Are vampires truly...dead?"

"In a sense, yes," Andreas replied, recalling his training at Mount Athos. As an apprentice demon slayer, he had been taught the nature of countless demons and their fiends—vampires, werewolves, sirens, and creatures far worse. "While they can live for centuries, there is no true life in them. It is as though their bodies endure, but their souls are neither in Hades nor Paradise. They are trapped, cursed to remain in this world forever."

"Or at least until someone cuts their head off," Andras added with an air of nonchalance, as though commenting on the weather.

"Is that how a vampire is killed?"

"Among other ways. Burning works, too. Though, amusingly, some vampires have been known to wield fire as their own weapon. The nature of vampires can be quite contrary, you see."

"How can we understand their abilities?"

The Deathchaser tittered. *"Why, by introducing ourselves, of course!"*

Andreas descended the hill. The villa's entry courtyard lay below: a broad expanse overgrown with wild, unkempt grass. A stone path snaked its way to the main gate, flanked by statues that had once depicted Roman gods and goddesses. Their faces, however, had been defaced, the features gouged and chipped. The act seemed deliberate, an affront to whatever sanctity the statues once held.

Near the gate lay a cluster of pale, bloodless corpses, their expressions locked in the terror they must have felt before death. The putrid stench of their rotting flesh assailed Andreas's nostrils.

"Must have been the previous owner and his servants," Andras said.

"Why leave them here?" Decimus asked.

"A warning, perhaps?" Andras mused. *"Or maybe the vampires have a penchant for the aroma of death. Either way, be grateful you're in the black meadow, my dear Decimus. You don't have to smell it."*

Andreas stopped before the villa's imposing iron gate. He reached for the handle, and as he did—

The skies, which had been clear and bright only moments ago, darkened suddenly. It wasn't the soft veil of dusk or the gradual deepening of evening, either. It was as dark as—

"Is this...the night?" Decimus said.

It was, or at least it appeared to be. Stars even sparkled overhead. Something resembling a half-moon hung brightly.

Andreas stepped back, then retreated from the villa's grounds, and as soon as his foot crossed the threshold, the world shifted again. The skies were blue and sunny once more.

He stepped forward again, crossing the invisible boundary into the villa's grounds. The transformation was instantaneous. The sun vanished, and the night descended completely.

"Well, then," the Deathchaser said. *"It seems one of the vampires can manipulate space—perhaps even time itself. Impressive."*

Demons, too, were capable of such feats. They could turn gentle rain into acid, change benign fog into poison, and even transform day into night. But this perpetual night gave the vampires a decisive advantage, amplifying their aether.

The light from the imitation half-moon cast many shadows over the entry courtyard. Andreas waited a moment, allowing his eyes to adjust to the darkness.

Then he approached the gate anew. Once more, he reached for the gate's handle.

"Behind you, my boy!"

A sharp whistling cut through the air. Andreas drew his lahat chereb and something metallic ricocheted off the black blade with a resonant clang. The object exploded into a puff of gray smoke.

Andreas had caught only a fleeting glimpse of the object: it was a small dagger, no larger than the breadth of a hand.

"Well done, demon slayer," a voice called out, chillingly calm and detached.

Andreas pulled on Andras's dark aether, expanding his awareness. He searched for the source of the voice, for any flicker of movement in the shadows.

Nothing.

"Who are you? Show yourself."

"I'm right here."

The voice came from behind him.

Andreas whirled around, his sword raised and ready, and was confronted with his assailant.

XIV

The man stood hunched, his pale skin stretched thin over angular bones and his dark purple lips a thin line. Long black hair hung over his face, obscuring much of his expression, but what could be seen revealed lifeless eyes like those of a corpse. Gradually, he unraveled the black cloak that enmeshed him like a cocoon. Beneath, he wore a black tunic, fitted to his gaunt frame. Belts crisscrossed his body, each bristling with an arsenal of daggers.

He clapped his hands as though in congratulations. "Very few could block my daggers the way you have."

"Fabian, I presume?"

"So you've heard of me. No doubt from Marcia. After I'm done with you, I'll deal with her and free Agrippa and Dosia."

"Is this darkness your doing?" Andreas gestured to the sky. False stars glittered and the pale imitation of a moon hung stagnant.

"The perpetual night? No. Only Valen possesses such powers."

"And where is Valen?" There was no sign of another foe. "Why is he not here with you?"

Fabian straightened slightly, his daggers ringing against each other. "I am more than capable of dealing with the likes of you, demon slayer."

Without another word, Fabian stepped back. As he moved, the shadows themselves seemed to shift, reaching out to engulf him. In an instant, he was gone.

Andreas remained still, his senses heightened, his body coiled like a spring. He hadn't fled. Fabian was still here, somewhere, hiding in the black abyss of shadow.

"Andras," Andreas muttered under his breath, "any thoughts?"

The demon's growling laughter reverberated through his mind. *"Oh, my boy, you're in for quite the game. Let's see if this vampire can survive your wrath."*

Andreas took a slow step forward, his blade raised, the faint glow of the sword's holy flames pushing back against the encroaching darkness. Fabian wouldn't remain hidden for long.

Andreas sensed movement and spun around, summoning the holy flames of his lahat chereb. Fabian leapt from the shadows, his dagger aimed at Andreas, who blocked Fabian's dagger with the flaming sword in a shower of sparks. The force of their collision created a small shock wave that sent both combatants skidding back several paces.

Again, Fabian dissolved into the shadows as if they were an extension of himself. He reappeared in the blink of an eye, hurling a dagger. Then, in a blur, he vanished again, materializing from another angle to repeat his assault. The daggers came unceasingly, each aiming for Andreas's vital points.

Andreas drew deeply on the Deathchaser's dark aether, enhancing his reflexes. The world slowed, every dagger's trajectory clear as he swung his flaming sword to intercept them. The blade burned through the air with a scorching hiss. Yet, for every dagger he deflected, another was hurled from an unpredictable direction.

His daggers were not ordinary daggers. Each time one struck the lahat chereb, it evaporated into a cloud of smoke. But there was no pause in Fabian's attack, no limit to his arsenal. There was a good chance the daggers were supernatural and Fabian's supply infinite.

Which did not bode well for Andreas.

***

In the black meadow, Andras stood with his arms crossed, his black cloak blowing wildly in the winds caused by the use of his aether.

"Your disciple uses the shadows to move quickly," the Deathchaser said to Decimus, glaring at the portal, watching as Andreas defended himself. "Though he is a coward for hiding like a rat."

Decimus was dumbfounded. The vampire resembled the man Decimus had first met years ago—sullen and withdrawn—but he was darker, more twisted, a macabre parody of his former self. Before joining Decimus's church, Fabian had been poor in spirit, mournful, and lost. Yet the teachings of Jesus Christ had ignited a spark of hope within him.

Now, that light had been snuffed out, and Fabian was a kind of dark apparition, lost in the shadows he had once craved.

Decimus clasped his hands together in prayer. The weather of the black meadow grew tumultuous and angry. Fierce winds howled, and fires erupted spontaneously across the field, their unholy flames defying the torrential rain that fell in heavy sheets.

"Oh, Fabian. May the Lord have mercy on you."

***

The daggers kept coming, darting at Andreas. There was no discernible pattern to Fabian's attacks. Wherever shadows lingered, Fabian could be also, and all in a flash. The darkness not only enhanced his vampiric power, but the darkness also *was* his power.

Andreas stayed on the defensive, though the unpredictability of Fabian's strikes was wearing him down. *Think, Andreas. Fight smarter.*

If only Andreas could get rid of the darkness somehow—

Could he use his sword?

He pulled on the sword's holy aether with greater need. The righteous flames burned within him and he gritted his teeth against the pain. He twirled his sword around, deflecting more of Fabian's daggers, and then, with the flames of the sword roaring, Andreas drove the sword into the earth.

The righteous fire erupted outward in a searing explosion of blue light. The darkness was momentarily obliterated. Everything around them was bathed in holy light, exposing Fabian.

No more hiding. No more shadowed refuge.

For the first time, Andreas saw the vampire clearly. Fabian's face was pale and hollow. He raised his daggers defensively, momentarily blinded by the intense light.

Andreas charged after him, his flaming sword poised for a decisive strike.

But Fabian unleashed a flurry of daggers, the projectiles hissing through the air. Andreas dodged, deflecting some with his sword, but the flurry seemed unending. One dagger slipped past his defense and slashed across his thigh. Hot pain seared through his leg, and he stumbled.

Fabian seized the opportunity—he dashed towards Andreas like a predator sensing weakness, his dagger aimed for Andreas's throat.

"Get up, my boy! Use the flames!"

Andreas roared as he swung his sword in a sweeping arc, unleashing a wave of holy fire. The flames licked the walls of the villa's courtyard and consumed the shadows. The heat was intense, the flames blinding, and Fabian staggered, thrown off balance as he barely avoided the attack.

Seeing his opening, Andreas charged. His hand slipped into the pouch at his side and closed around one of the wooden crosses Marcia had given him. He hoped its sanctity would paralyze Fabian as it had Agrippa and Dosia.

But as he lunged forward to press the cross against Fabian's chest, the vampire was yanked away and Andreas missed his chance.

Fabian didn't vanish into the shadows—few were left now, as the courtyard blazed with holy flames. Instead, he had been spirited away, and now he stood at the villa's entrance, the iron doors towering behind him.

And he was not alone.

Another vampire was with him, this one exuding an aether that made even Andreas shudder.

"It's him," Decimus said. *"It's Valen."*

XV

"You must be Valen," Andreas said, forcing himself to take slow, measured breaths to calm his racing heart and trembling limbs. The holy flames faded away from the lahat chereb, the sword having taken its toll on him.

His thigh throbbed where Fabian's dagger had cut. Blood trickled down his leg.

Valen bowed, a sardonic smile across his blackened lips. His piercing yellow eyes were shadowed and looked at Andreas with quiet confidence. He wore the armor of a Roman soldier, a black cape flowing behind him. He had no sword, or any weapon for that matter, that Andreas could see. The nails on his fingers were long and pointed, and the veins on his neck, arms, and hands pulsed with what Andreas could only describe as eagerness—an eagerness to be filled with blood.

"And you must be the demon slayer," Valen said in a low, powerful voice, "though you will find no demons here, Andreas."

Andreas narrowed his gaze. How did Valen know his name?

"Likely," the Deathchaser supplied, *"he is connected to Agrippa and Dosia. As their maker, he would know everything they know."*

If that were true, then Valen already understood Andreas's methods, his weaknesses, and the holy relics he had used to incapacitate the other vampires. It explained why Valen had spirited Fabian away during their earlier battle. Clearly, Fabian, like the others, was vulnerable to the cross.

Andreas would remember that.

Valen raised a hand and Andreas tensed, expecting an attack. None came. Instead, dark clouds above churned, and moments later, heavy rain began to fall. Once the smoldering flames around the courtyard were extinguished, Valen lowered his hand, and the rain slowed, then stopped entirely. Droplets clung to his black cape and armor.

Then Valen went for the iron gate and pulled it open. He stepped back and gestured towards the inside. "Won't you come in, Andreas?"

"Careful, my boy. I smell a trap."

Decimus's voice followed. *"But my daughter is in there. I know it."*

Andreas couldn't turn back now—not when Cassia might be just beyond those doors. He would have to press on. It seemed Valen had no wish to fight. Yet. It might be Andreas's only opportunity to regain some of his strength before the inevitable.

"I mean you no harm," Valen assured, spreading his hands wide. "As you can see, I am unarmed."

That did not mean he was harmless.

Nevertheless, Andreas sheathed the black sword. Then he tore a strip of fabric from his cloak and tied it around his wounded thigh, staunching the bleeding.

"Fabian, leave us," Valen commanded.

Fabian bristled. "But—"

A single dark look from Valen silenced the younger vampire. Fabian recoiled like a scolded dog, then bowed.

"Of course, master."

Into the shadows Fabian went, disappearing as he had during their battle. Andreas had no doubt, however, that Fabian would continue to follow unseen, lurking in the villa's darkness, awaiting his master's next order.

For whatever reason, Valen wanted to play the gracious host. It was as if the vampire saw Andreas not as a threat but as a foreign dignitary visiting the court of the self-proclaimed blood prince. Valen seemed eager to uphold the decorum of a host.

Andreas steeled himself and stepped through the entryway and into the villa's atrium.

Inside, it was deathly quiet, broken only by the faint sound of rainwater dripping from his soaked cloak. Valen followed close behind, closing the iron door behind them.

It was pitch black. Andreas's hand went to the pommel of his sword.

Valen snapped his fingers, and with a sudden whoosh, the torches lining the walls ignited in unison. The flickering flames lit dreary corridors. The air was thick with the stench of rot, strong enough to churn the stomach of most men. But Andreas was no stranger to the smell of death and ruin. Spiders scuttled across the cracked stone walls while centipedes writhed and twisted along the marble floors.

"Come," Valen said. "Let me show you my villa."

The vampire escorted Andreas through the halls, leading him through a labyrinth of chambers and corridors. There was a study with walls lined with shelves of scrolls and manuscripts, their edges yellowed and curling. The dining room was an abomination, the long wooden table laden with spoiled food, buzzing with flies.

The kitchen was cavernous but empty, its hearth cold and lifeless. In contrast, the bathhouses, separated into rooms for cold, warm, and hot baths, retained a strange sense of their former luxury, though cobwebs draped the tiled walls.

Finally, they came to a small shrine dedicated to Roman gods. The statues had been shattered, their fragmented pieces strewn across the floor. Andreas stepped over a broken marble hand.

The faint scent of blood lingered in the air, clinging to every corner of the villa.

"Why did you kill the previous owners and take their home?" Andreas asked.

"I am the Blood Prince," Valen said. "I could not live among my subjects. And I needed to be close to my temple."

No doubt Valen referred to the structure that Decimus had once claimed as a church, a place that had been devoted to the blood goddess Absalona.

“You see yourself as some kind of god?”

Valen chuckled. “Was it not Jesus who said we are gods?”

Jesus had quoted Psalm 82 when he said those words. His intent had been to emphasize that His title as the Son of God held unparalleled significance because He was the one God the Father had chosen and sent to defeat death, heal sin, and conquer demons. It was a profound statement meant to inspire faith, showing that mankind, through Jesus, could share in divine grace and reflect the image of the Creator.

It did not mean what Valen implied: that he himself was a god equal to or above the Most High.

Such a claim was not only blasphemy but a perversion of everything Jesus had taught, everything his disciples had recorded, and everything Andreas had sworn to defend with his life.

Andreas glared at Valen. “You will pay for what you’ve done—to them, to the villagers, and to the priest.”

In the face of such animosity, Valen only smiled. “Ah, yes, Father Decimus. I suppose you think I hate him.

But the truth is, I am grateful to him. Without him, I would not be who I am today. When I was a Christian, as he preached, I sought new life. And he was right—I have found it."

"This is not the life I envisioned for him or anyone in my congregation," Decimus said, regret in his tone. *"I never wanted it to come to this. How was I to know?"*

Decimus had only been doing his best to lead his flock toward salvation. But what had his efforts wrought? A monster like Valen, standing here in defiance of everything Decimus believed in.

"Now." Valen gestured towards a set of stairs. "Let me show you the second floor."

As Andreas followed Valen up the creaky steps, he asked, "How are you able to make the day into night?"

"One of my many abilities. I create a sphere around the villa, and within that sphere, I can manipulate the space as I please."

It was a thinly veiled threat, meant to remind Andreas of the vampire's power; to emphasize that here, in this distorted space, Valen reigned supreme.

"It's like a Circle of Hades," the Deathchaser said.

Surely there were limitations to Valen's ability to manipulate the sphere around the villa. If his power were absolute, he could have simply closed the sphere in on Andreas, crushing him with invisible walls, or found a way to trap him here forever. Even a Circle of Hades crafted by a demon prince had its weaknesses. The challenge was identifying that weakness and exploiting it.

They reached the second floor, where Valen began to show Andreas the bedrooms. Though the rooms had been lavishly decorated with fine rugs and ornate tapestries, neglect over the past weeks had left them dusty and stale.

"What is it that you hope to achieve as this blood prince?"

Valen stopped in front of a tall window with broken shutters, gazing out into the distorted darkness of his domain. "What do you know of these lands, Andreas?"

"I am not from here, if that is what you're asking."

"No, I wouldn't think so." He turned to Andreas. "The Romans took these lands for their empire. They massacred the people here. The land calls out to me for vengeance. I seek to build an army and make Rome pay for what it has done."

His story was not uncommon. The Roman Empire had conquered many lands, killing tens of thousands. Many plotted against the Empire, yet few succeeded.

Rome's strength lay not only in its legions but in its partnership with demonic forces.

No army of farmers or fledgling vampires could ever hope to topple the Empire's might. Even the demon slayers of Mount Athos, despite their skill, could not hope to cut through the legions of demons that bolstered Rome's power.

"But you yourself are Roman, aren't you? You were even a soldier."

"I was. It's true. But I deserted. If you seek demons, Andreas, you need not look far. Go to Rome, and you will find demons aplenty to satisfy your sword's hunger."

"Is your plan to make the villagers into an army of vampires?"

Valen nodded. "Some will become vampires. Others will serve."

Serve how? As cattle to be bled dry?

There was also something unsettling in the way Valen spoke—as though the plan weren't entirely his own. His words carried the weight of a mouthpiece, not a mastermind. Was he acting on behalf of someone else?

Absalona, perhaps? Did she harbor a grudge against Rome? Was Valen merely her pawn in a grander, darker scheme?

"And how does Cassia fit within your plan?"

"She is my bride, my princess, my queen," Valen said. "She will be at my side as we make the streets of Rome run red with blood."

"Did you turn her?"

"No. She remains a mortal."

"Thank God!" Decimus exclaimed, and Andreas could feel the priest's relief.

"Is she safe?" Andreas asked.

"Of course, she is," Valen said, his tone almost offended by the implication. Then, with a dramatic flair, he gestured to a nearby hallway. "Would you like to see her?"

Andreas nodded. "I would."

Valen led him down a dim corridor to a single closed door, a stark contrast to the open and neglected rooms Andreas had seen throughout the villa.

"She's through here," Valen said, his fingers curling around the iron handle. He pushed the door open, revealing a bedroom that benefited from a wide balcony with a view of the Adriatic Sea.

A simple chair was positioned before the view, and in it sat a woman, her back turned to them. Her figure was still, and she did not turn around as Andreas stepped into the room.

"Cassia," Andreas said.

She did not respond. She didn't even move.

"Go on, demon slayer," Valen said from the doorway. "She won't bite," he added as his own fangs pointed out from his upper lip.

XVI

Andreas moved to stand in front of the woman seated in the chair. Her posture was oddly rigid, her hands resting in her lap.

In his mind, Decimus gasped.

"It's her. It's my daughter. Oh, thank the Lord!"

Andreas scrutinized her closely. There was no mistaking her identity: this was indeed Cassia. But something was wrong. Her body was here, tangible and real. Yet her vacant gaze troubled him. She didn't look up at him, didn't flinch or even acknowledge his presence. Her eyes stared straight ahead, blank and unfocused, as though she were gazing into another world entirely. It was likely she didn't even register the view of the Adriatic Sea beyond the balcony.

"Free her, Andreas! Please! I beg of you!"

But there were no physical bindings. No chains, no ropes. She could have stood and walked out of the room herself, and yet she remained eerily still.

"As you can see," Valen said, "she has no bite marks on her neck, and she is not a vampire. Her heart beats the same as any mortal's heart. She is my bride, and I would not hurt her."

Andreas knelt down. "Cassia? Can you hear me?"

No response. A trail of drool slipped from the corner of her mouth.

"I don't understand," Decimus said. *"What's wrong with her?"*

"Perhaps she suffers from a glamor," the Deathchaser offered.

"A glamor?"

It's an ability vampires use to enchant mortals, Andreas explained silently, *to force them to do their bidding.*

"Unfortunately," Andras added, *"it can rot the mind if used for too long."*

"You mean—"

Andreas got to his feet and glared at Valen. "Release your glamor."

Valen snickered. "Glamor? Oh, Andreas, there is no glamor at work here. I wouldn't even know how to glamor her—or any other mortal, for that matter. She became like this when I took her."

"After my death. Perhaps she's in shock?"

"No," the Deathchaser said. *"There is something else at work here. Something...demonic."*

Andreas could sense it, too. A demonic presence penetrated the room—a pulse to the air like that of blood pumping through veins. And a faint smell of iron.

"She isn't normal," Andreas said. He searched Valen's expression for any sign of understanding. "You must see that."

"I beg to differ, demon slayer. She is obedient. She will not run from me. She is mine, for as long as I want her." He gestured toward her as though she were a trophy on display. "As you can see, Cassia is safe. Shall we leave her in peace? Perhaps take a walk to the garden?"

"Where is Absalona?"

At the mention of the name, Valen's brow furrowed. His expression shifted into genuine confusion. "Pardon me, Andreas, but who is this Absalona?"

No guile in his tone; not even a hint of a lie. He truly didn't know who Absalona was.

"He's lying to you, Andreas. Tell him to bring back my little girl!"

"Quiet, priest!" Andras snarled *"My boy, Valen may be telling the truth, but that doesn't mean Absalona isn't involved somehow."*

Doubtless, she was. The pulse of the demonic presence all but confirmed it.

"Who made you a vampire?" Andreas asked Valen.

Valen shrugged. "I awoke this way after my death. I became what you see in front of you. Dead, but alive; alive, but dead."

But all vampires had a maker, and the original source always traced back to a demon. Vampires could then spread their curse to others by mixing their blood with the dying. Mortals simply didn't wake up as vampires without a cause.

So which was it for Valen? Was another vampire his maker? Or was it something more sinister—a demon, perhaps Absalona herself, posing as a goddess to grant him this unholy existence?

"I don't know what you are driving at, demon slayer," Valen said, his voice tinged with annoyance. "But I do not appreciate your line of questioning. I've brought you into my home and treated you as an honored guest. I have shown you that Cassia is unharmed. Yet you insist on this...rudeness. I will not tolerate it further. I must insist that you leave immediately."

Andreas had grown tired of Valen's pretense of civility. "Very well," he said. "But I'm taking Cassia with me."

Valen smiled mirthlessly. "I think not."

Andreas reached for Cassia. As his hand extended, crystalline walls materialized around her, forming an impenetrable barrier. Andreas laid his hand flat against the cold, glass-like surface.

"I told you, didn't I?" Valen said. "This place is mine. I can shape it as I see fit."

Andreas drew his sword.

Valen sighed dramatically, his shoulders rising and falling with exaggerated disappointment. "I see. So you have chosen violence, then. I suppose I should have expected it. I had hoped, perhaps foolishly, that you would join my cause. A man of your skills would have been invaluable. But no matter." He spread his arms wide, dark aether rippling from his form. "I will bring you to the brink of death, demon slayer. And then I will make you one of mine."

And the room began to shift around them.

XVII

The villa morphed and transformed into a sprawling hall with marble columns adorned with flickering torchlight. Shadows loomed long over the stone floors.

Andreas stood near the center of the hall, his gaze locked on Valen.

Gone was the view of the Adriatic. They were no longer on the second floor of the villa. The villa had been remade into a battleground.

Cassia was nowhere to be seen.

Valen stood confidently, a smile curling at the edge of his lips. Arrogance glinted in his vampiric eyes. Andreas ignited his lahat chereb, the blue flames dancing wildly.

"Do you like what I've done with the place?" Valen asked, spreading his arms to emphasize the majesty of his creation. "This hall is a reflection of my will. A space where I am king, and you, demon slayer, are nothing more than prey."

The Deathchaser's voice rumbled in Andreas's mind. *"My boy, you should flee. There's no telling what he can do here—and you're injured."*

Andreas shifted his weight, wincing at the pain in his thigh. The fabric he had tied around the wound was soaked through, the blood loss beginning to wear on him. Normally, the wound would be manageable, but the lahat chereb's holy flames worsened the pain.

But retreat wasn't an option. The hall was enclosed completely. Like a coffin.

From the corner of his eye, the shadows beside him quivered and a dagger flashed toward his throat.

Sparks erupted as the dagger clashed with the flaming blade, the sound ringing in the enclosed space. Fabian emerged briefly from the shadows, his pale face devoid of emotion, before retreating into the dark, vanishing once more.

Valen lifted his hands. The marble walls shuddered, warping and elongating, throwing Andreas off balance. The floor seemed to tilt beneath his boots, though when he steadied himself, he realized it hadn't moved at all. The room itself was playing tricks, as if the entire space had become an enemy.

"Impressive, isn't it?" Valen remarked. "A battleground where even the environment will see to your undoing."

Fabian's haunting laughter echoed through the hall as he darted between the long shadows, throwing dagger after dagger at Andreas. Drawing on the Deathchaser's aether, Andreas moved with supernatural reflexes, dodging and deflecting Fabian's projectiles. The unrelenting barrage forced him onto the defensive.

"Stop playing their game, my boy!" Andras urged. *"You won't win this way. Think of an advantage. Create one if you must!"*

Andreas dropped to a crouch, dodging another volley of daggers. Fabian's derisive laughter echoed again, but Andreas wasn't going to stay on the defensive any longer. Gritting his teeth against the pain in his leg, he launched himself forward, closing the distance between him and the shadows.

Fabian appeared just long enough to throw another dagger before slipping back into the darkness. Each time Andreas neared, the vampire vanished, always just out of reach.

"You'll tire soon, demon slayer," Fabian taunted, his voice carrying an icy edge. "And when you do, I'll bleed you dry."

Andreas ignored the words, forcing himself to focus. His breaths came heavily, his movements slowing under the weight of exhaustion and injury, but his determination didn't waver.

"Enough," Andreas growled. The flames of his sword flared brighter, illuminating the grotesque hall. "I'll drag you into the light if I must."

The words were a promise. One way or another, Fabian would be forced into the open. And once he was, Andreas would strike.

"Remember, Andreas, not to hurt Fabian!" Decimus said.

Another complication. Another obstacle. Andreas gritted his teeth. Fine. If he could incapacitate Fabian using Marcia's cross, he could eliminate one threat and focus entirely on Valen.

"Very well, priest," the Deathchaser sneered, *"but Valen dies. This time for good."*

The demon's bloodlust stirred within Andreas.

Valen waved his hands through the air. The walls of the hall stretched further and the ceiling rose to impossible heights. The ground tilted beneath Andreas and he staggered. A dagger whistled past him, nicking his cheek and leaving a stinging line of blood.

Before Andreas's very eyes, the blood prince melted into a swirling, viscous mist that swept overhead like a predatory cloud.

From the mist Valen had shapeshifted into, his imperious voice boomed, "There is nowhere to run, demon slayer. Nowhere to hide. I am everywhere."

If that was true, then there was only one option left. Andreas gripped the lahat chereb with both hands, summoning more of the sword's aether.

With a powerful cry, he swung the sword repeatedly. Blue flames tore through the warped space, burning away the edges of Valen's manipulation and illuminating the shadows.

The mist of Valen's form recoiled from the flames, unable to maintain its dominance. Meanwhile, Fabian, who had relied on the cover of shadows, found himself suddenly exposed.

Andreas seized the opportunity. Within a heartbeat, he closed the gap between them, removed Marcia's cross from his pouch, and planted it on Fabian's chest.

The reaction was instantaneous. Fabian's scream tore through the hall, high-pitched and anguished. The vampire crumpled to his knees, his strength utterly drained. He writhed on the fractured ground, helpless under the cross's innate power.

Valen roared in fury, his form blurring as he shapeshifted. His body contorted and expanded, transforming into a towering wolf with fur as black as midnight and eyes as gold as a crown fit for an emperor. The massive beast snarled, its fangs bared, saliva dripping from its maw.

With a thunderous growl, Valen lunged at Andreas. The sheer force of his charge sent a gust of wind rippling through the hall. Claws slashed through the air.

Andreas raised his lahat chereb, the black blade meeting Valen's claws in a resounding clash. Sparks ignited between them. The ground beneath them trembled with each strike, the force of their battle threatening to tear the space apart.

Now that Fabian was incapacitated, Andreas poured all his focus into Valen. He sent a scorching wave of blue flames hurtling toward Valen. The fire struck true, engulfing Valen's fur. The monstrous wolf howled in agony, and Valen was forced to revert to his form as a man.

Smoke rose from Valen's smoldering armor. His confidence remained unshaken, as though Andreas's efforts were nothing more than an inconvenience. He formed a Roman gladius from the marble of the floor and began tracing signs in the air with his free hand.

The entire hall quaked fiercely. Dust and debris cascaded from the dizzyingly high ceiling. The floor groaned as cracks spiderwebbed across it. Sections of the floor rose into jagged peaks while others sank into ominous depths.

The walls buckled and began closing in, narrowing the space.

"Finish him now, my boy!"

Andreas surged forward, the combined energies of the lahat chereb and the dark power of the Deathchaser coursing through his veins like a storm. The two opposing forces clashed within him, searing both his body and mind.

The space around him buckled. Platforms floated in a chaotic void, some crumbling as soon as his boots touched them. Gaping chasms yawned beneath him, and the air was thick with heat and pressure. Walls slammed together in a rhythmic, bone-crushing dance, a deadly obstacle threatening to end him with a single misstep.

Andreas leapt from one precarious platform to the next, his sword ablaze. He clenched his jaw, his muscles screaming in protest as he pushed himself harder and faster.

Nearly there.

Just a little more—

He launched himself from the final platform, the momentum of his leap carrying him straight toward Valen. The vampire's golden eyes widened in shock, a rare crack in his arrogant composure. Valen raised his gladius in a desperate attempt to block the oncoming strike.

It was futile.

The lahat chereb met Valen's gladius and sliced through it effortlessly. The blade seared through the vampire's armor, plunging deep into his chest.

Valen let out a half scream as the flames consumed him from the inside out. His flesh blackened and crumbled to ash, the cursed light of his golden eyes dimming until they were extinguished entirely.

Valen, the self-proclaimed blood prince, was no more.

XVIII

"It's over," Decimus said. *"This nightmare is finally over."*

They had returned to the second floor of the villa. The perpetual night had vanished, replaced with the light of late morning. The golden rays of the sun poured through the room's wide balcony, bathing everything in a warm glow. The light fell upon Cassia, who remained seated in her chair, the barrier that had surrounded her now gone.

Andreas took a moment to catch his breath. His wounds burned from using too much of the dark and holy aether. He sheathed his black sword, the flames now faded.

At his feet lay a small, scattered pile of ashes—the last remnants of Valen. The vampire's shattered gladius rested beside the ashes.

Behind him, a faint stirring drew his attention. Fabian groaned, his body shifting as the cross that had been planted on his chest slipped free and fell to the floor with a dull thud.

Andreas approached him, kneeling beside the young man to assess his condition. Fabian's once-pale skin had deepened into a healthy olive tone, and the sharp fangs that had marked him as a vampire were gone.

"It worked," Decimus said. *"Oh, thank the Lord! Fabian is saved!"*

Fabian's eyes fluttered open as though he were waking from a long, fitful dream. He groaned again, attempting to push himself upright.

"Who are you? Where am I?"

"I'm Andreas, a demon slayer of Mount Athos," Andreas said. "What do you remember?"

With Andreas's help, Fabian rose to his feet.

"I...I was in a dark room," Fabian said haltingly. "Everything was black. It robbed me of my senses. And I remember..." He looked down at his hands, turning them over as if they belonged to someone else.

The realization passed through him and his mouth quivered. "Oh, God, what have I done?"

Andreas placed a steady hand on his shoulder, grounding him. "Valen made you into a vampire, but the curse has been lifted. You are free now."

"Where is Valen?"

"He is no more," Andreas replied simply.

Fabian shook his head. "But I've done terrible things." He covered his face with his hands, ashamed. "Awful, awful things."

Andreas gently pulled Fabian's hands away from his face. The boy—he was just a boy, no older than fourteen summers—looked back at him with an expression of raw vulnerability.

"God will show you mercy," Andreas said. "Are you hurt anywhere?"

"No. At least I don't think so." He paused, then added quietly, "T-thank you, demon slayer."

Andreas nodded.

"What about my Cassia?" Decimus implored. *"Is she, too, saved?"*

Andreas turned to the priest's daughter. She had not moved or spoken since Valen's demise, but as though she could hear her father's voice, she slowly stood up from the creaking chair, the motion almost mechanical.

She turned to face them. Her hands fell to her sides, and her expression remained blank, devoid of the joy or relief one might expect from someone freed from captivity.

Was it shock? Guilt?

According to Valen, she was neither a vampire nor under a glamor. She was still mortal, still herself. She had been held captive and now, by all appearances, was free.

Yet she didn't look like a girl who had just escaped a nightmare.

"Cassia! My dear, dear daughter!" Decimus cried. *"She's alive and well! She's free!"*

Cassia stepped forward and stopped at the ashes. Ignoring the ashes, she crouched down and picked up the broken gladius. Rising to her full height, she stared at the sword with a quiet fascination, tilting it as though appraising its edge.

"Cassia?" Fabian said, stepping closer. Relief flooded his face as he stretched his arms toward her. "I'm so glad you're safe."

"Something isn't right, my boy."

Andreas sensed it, too. A chilling presence, distinct from the aura of any vampire.

Demonic.

Cassia's lips curved up into a grin, but it wasn't one of relief or recognition. It was a bloodthirsty, cruel expression that sent a jolt of dread through Andreas.

"Wait!" Andreas lunged forward, but it was too late.

In a blur of movement, Cassia swiped with the broken gladius; what blade it had left slashed across Fabian's throat. Blood splattered on Cassia, soaking her garments in crimson.

Fabian staggered, his hands clutching at his throat in a futile attempt to stem the torrent of blood. He crumpled to the ground, his wide eyes locked in disbelief.

She stood over him, the broken sword still in her hand, her grin widening, her eyes glowing with malice.

ACT THREE

I

How could a ghost feel such dread?

The horrible feeling manifested inside of Decimus; in his heart, if ghosts had such things. To witness his daughter slit the throat of poor Fabian was his worst nightmare. It was worse than whatever fate awaited him in Hades should the scavenger demons steal his soul.

"What in Heavens is going on?" Decimus said. Questions ran through his mind with no clear answers. "Isn't the curse lifted? Why would Cassia—"

He couldn't even bring himself to say it.

"Haven't you guessed, my dear Decimus?" Andras rasped. He appeared drained after the battle with Valen; his eyes were sunken, his cheeks hollow, his posture slouched. "Valen was nothing but a pawn. Your daughter is the true transgressor here."

"But she's not a vampire," Decimus protested.

Even Valen had claimed as much. If she wasn't a vampire, then—

"She's demon-possessed," the Deathchaser stated flatly.

Decimus clenched his jaw, fighting off a wave of nausea. Could a ghost be sick in the black meadow? How could a ghost like himself feel such corporeal sensations?

For how long had this demon plagued his daughter? What vile force could have taken her?

"My boy," Andras said to Andreas, "you must flee. You're injured, and my aether is nearly depleted. We have no idea what this demon is capable of, but it's clear you cannot face her. Not yet."

"Fight her?" Decimus said and clung to Andras's arm. "You would fight Cassia? But you're meant to save her!"

The Deathchaser scowled. "Look at her, priest. Does she look like the Cassia you once knew?"

She did not. With Fabian's blood nearly covering her from head to toe, the gentle girl who had once prayed beside him, who had laughed at the smallest joys, was nowhere to be found.

"But there must be a way!" Decimus squeezed Andras's arm. "An exorcism or—"

Andras yanked his arm free. "I'm afraid it's too late. The demon has her. Completely. Your daughter is gone."

***

"You slew my champion, demon slayer," hissed the demon inside of Cassia, her voice not at all what a fourteen-year-old should sound like. "He was mine. I would have made him a great prince of this world."

Fabian's body lay crumpled on the floor, his blood pooling around him. His fingers twitched once before going completely limp. He did not deserve such a grim fate. Andreas had saved him from his vampirism but had failed to save his life.

"Are you the demon Absalona?" Andreas asked.

Cassia cocked her head. "Demon? No. I am a goddess. I am older than Rome. I am older than even your Christ."

Christ was the Word made flesh; in the beginning was the Word, and the Word was with God, and the Word was God. Before Adam, before the foundations of the earth, Jesus Christ was. Even demons acknowledged this fundamental truth, and yet Absalona dared to deny it.

"Perhaps, my boy, she is one of the children of the sons of God."

The sons of God. The elohim who had once served Yahweh but, seduced by lust, had taken mortal women as their wives. Their unholy unions produced creatures neither fully man nor divine—demigods, monsters, and abominations. When those beings perished, their spirits lingered on the earth, becoming the demons that tormented mankind.

It explained why Andras had never heard of Absalona before. She was not a demon prince, but dangerous nonetheless, for these demons had inherited the aetheric abilities of their divine fathers.

"Why did you choose Cassia?"

"She called to me," the demon said. "She wanted me. She was weak and needed me."

Andreas's heart sank. *She called to me.* The words gnawed at him. He had known of Cassia's history—how she had lost her mother and been uprooted from her life in the city to accompany her father to a remote village. There, Decimus had devoted himself entirely to building his church, glorifying the Lord. Was it possible that, in his fervor, he had unintentionally neglected his grieving, lonely daughter? Had her pain and isolation created the void that allowed this vile entity to take root in her soul?

Andreas understood that feeling. His mother, a zealot for a demonic cult, had inflicted years of abuse upon him. It was that pain, that vulnerability, that had allowed Andras the Deathchaser to possess him.

Andreas's resolve hardened. He would not abandon Cassia to the same fate. She needed to know she was not alone, that she didn't have to surrender herself to this malevolent force to fill the wounds in her heart.

"She is weak," Absalona said. "But she will suffice for now."

"You planned on possessing Valen?"

"No." She spat at Valen's ashes. "You would expect me to possess a filthy Roman? Never! He was to build my army. He was to worship me, to be my sword. But perhaps not all is lost."

"Come out of Cassia. With Valen dead, she's no use to you anymore. You said as much yourself."

"She is still mine, demon slayer. And I require her body."

Which meant Absalona was weak herself. Demons who fashioned themselves as gods thrived on the worship and sacrifices of mortals, feeding on their devotion to sustain their power. If she needed Cassia, it meant she lacked the strength to take a stronger host or act independently. Perhaps she could be defeated here and now, even in his battered and fatigued state.

But hurting Cassia was out of the question. Andreas had to force Absalona to leave her body without harming the girl.

"I need more," Absalona said. "More blood. I may have lost Valen, but I still have those who would worship me."

The Blood Militia. Doubtless, those zealots would willingly spill their blood for her. These so-called gods and demons demanded so much, their yokes unbearable for the mortals who served them.

"I won't let you hurt anyone else," Andreas said.

Absalona laughed, a grating, hollow sound. "Come now, demon slayer. We both know you won't harm this body. I may have been lost in the shadows of time, forgotten after Rome's massacre of my worshipers, but I know your kind. You cannot harm an innocent child."

"She's right, my boy."

Andreas thought otherwise. He drew the lahat chereb and summoned its flames.

"What are you doing, Andreas?" Decimus's voice trembled with fear. *"She's my daughter!"*

Absalona is weak, Andreas replied in his mind. *The sword's holy power should be enough to drive her out.*

"Truly?"

It's worth trying.

"But is it worth dying?" Andras interjected. *"The sword will consume you—and it will take me and Decimus with you."*

Andras was scared. In truth, so was Andreas.

But more importantly, so was Absalona.

Her eyes, wide with fear, watched the sword's flames flicker. She took a step back as Andreas leveled the blade at her heart.

"I can't let you harm anyone else," Andreas said. Unlike priests who were skilled and trained in exorcisms, demon slayers like him possessed only a working knowledge of how those rituals functioned. For most demon slayers, their guardian angel would perform an exorcism on their behalf. But Andreas was no ordinary demon slayer.

That made this situation infinitely more challenging. If only he had Felix, a young but talented exorcist from Mount Athos, by his side.

"I am warning you, Absalona," Andreas said, his tone sharp. "Come out of her. The Lord of Heaven and Earth commands it!"

Cassia—no, Absalona—laughed, her voice a chilling mixture of Cassia's and something far darker. It echoed unnaturally through the room.

"No!" she shrieked. "I will not! I have waited long enough, demon slayer! Now is my time! And neither you nor your God can stop me!"

She raised her right hand above her, fingers reaching for the ceiling. The blood covering her skin and soaked into her clothes slid upward, gathering along her arm and pooling into her palm.

The pool of blood Fabian lay in was drawn to her hand. Even the blood seeping from Andreas's wounds joined the crimson tide. The swirling mass coalesced into a hovering sphere of blood, pulsating with an otherworldly energy.

"In the state I am in now," she said, "I cannot hope to defeat you. But I still possess power enough to stop you."

Stop him? How?

Andreas didn't have the luxury of pondering that question. In one swift motion, Absalona hurled the blood sphere at him.

Andreas raised his flaming sword, ready to counter.

"No, my boy!" Andras bellowed. *"Don't let the blood touch you!"*

Too late—

Andreas's blade sliced through the sphere, and it exploded on contact, drenching him in a torrent of blood. The crimson liquid coated him from head to toe, seeping into every crevice of his armor. The vile substance burned his skin, stung his eyes, and flooded his mouth with its bitterness.

He gagged, spitting and coughing, trying desperately to expel the foul taste. The flames of the lahat chereb sputtered and died, leaving him vulnerable and defenseless.

Wiping frantically at his eyes, Andreas could only catch a fleeting glimpse of Absalona. She stood with an eerie calmness, a twisted smile playing across her lips.

Then, without a word, she turned her back to him and walked toward the balcony.

Red.

Red was all Andreas could see. The blood coated his vision, his thoughts, his everything.

II

"We were trapped in endless darkness," Dosia said, hugging herself. "It was cold, and we were alone. We couldn't move or speak. It was as though we were trapped in a sarcophagus."

"It must be what Hades is like," Agrippa added. His expression was gaunt, his eyes hollow.

The couple sat close together in the hay-strewn corner of the stable, visibly shaken. Their vampirism had been replaced with frailty. They were no longer predators but broken mortals, humbled and terrified.

Marcia had freed them earlier that morning, once it was clear their vampirism had reversed. They no longer craved blood nor even sought solace in each other's arms.

For Marcia, the sight was bittersweet. Relief washed over her to see them mortal again, but sorrow weighed down her heart as she witnessed their fragile state. What horrors they must have endured.

"Do you remember anything else?" Marcia asked, kneeling beside them on the hay-covered ground. The stable was quiet except for the occasional whinny of a horse. Warm sunlight streamed through the wooden slats.

Dosia reached out and gripped Marcia's hand. "Only that we could hear ourselves...and we knew what we had done as vampires. It was like being awake inside a nightmare you couldn't control." She paused, her eyes full of sorrow. "I'm sorry, Marcia. I said terrible things to you. I—"

Marcia smiled, seeking to comfort the girl. "It's over now. You're both safe. Thank God you're safe."

Andreas must have slain Valen, ending his reign as a vampire lord. Surely, that was why Dosia and Agrippa had been restored to their mortal selves. Soon Fabian and Cassia would join them in the village, and perhaps, they could all begin to rebuild their lives.

But rebuild to what?

They couldn't return to the lives they'd had before, not after everything that had happened. Decimus's death had shattered the foundation of their church and their sense of spiritual guidance.

"But we..." Agrippa faltered, lowering his gaze to the floor. "We committed such atrocious sins."

"It wasn't you," Marcia said gently. "God will forgive you, surely."

Did she fully understand the depths of forgiveness herself? She wasn't certain. Yet, she believed with all her heart that God's mercy was vast, capable of enveloping even the most wayward souls. The Lord, she knew, could see into the hearts of all mortals, judging them for who they truly were—whether sinner or saint.

"Forgiveness is yours," she continued, "if only you give your pain, sorrow, and regret to the Lord of Heaven. Only He can heal it."

Her words seemed to ease their suffering. The tension in Agrippa's shoulders relaxed, and Dosia wiped at her tear-streaked face. The faintest glimmer of hope began to take root in their expressions.

"You must rest," Marcia said, "and take food and drink."

"Is it true about Decimus?" Agrippa asked. "Has he...did Valen..."

Marcia nodded somberly. "I'm afraid so. But his soul has not yet departed the mortal world. He is helping the demon slayer even now."

She wondered if she would ever see Decimus again. It seemed unlikely. She had seen his spirit only once—when he had risked everything to come to her, urging her to summon for Andreas of Mount Athos.

Now, with Cassia rescued, Decimus's spirit would find rest. He would ascend to Paradise to join the Lord and his beloved wife, preparing for the Day of the Lord when all things would be made new.

"Then Valen is slain?" Dosia asked.

Marcia nodded. "Andreas will be returning soon. He'll bring Fabian and Cassia with him."

Dosia frowned. "Cassia will be heartbroken."

"She'll need us," Marcia said. "We're her family now. If we are there for her, we can help her through this difficult time. It won't be easy for any of us. Decimus was more than our priest—he was our spiritual father. We must pray for God's comfort and guidance."

"But the church..." Agrippa said, his voice trailing off as he glanced in the direction of the temple.

"We are still here. As long as we remain full of the Holy Spirit, we can spread the Gospel that Decimus taught us."

Decimus had always spoken of the resilience of the faithful, how the church was not bound by walls or the presence of a single leader. His teachings were etched into their hearts, and though they lacked a spiritual father now, they had each other. If they remained steadfast in prayer, fasting, and serving those in need, the light of the church would never fade from this village.

Dosia's lips curved into a small, sincere smile. "You've endured so much, Marcia, and yet your faith remains unshaken. You inspire me."

In truth, she was exhausted. She'd been living in constant fear for the past two weeks. She could collapse into the soft, earthy scent of the horse's hay and let sleep claim her for the rest of the day. But despite her weariness, she wanted to stay awake. Cassia would return soon, and Marcia yearned to greet her friend with open arms. And then there was the demon slayer. She owed him her thanks, though the words seemed so small compared to the magnitude of his deeds.

"It's over now," Marcia said. "That's what matters."

Even so, the Blood Militia remained a looming threat. Their blood prince might have fallen, but his demise didn't guarantee peace. Would they now leave on their own accord?

Raised voices and the clatter of hurried footsteps sounded outside.

Dosia stiffened. “What’s that noise?”

“Perhaps the demon slayer has returned,” Agrippa said.

Perhaps—but those voices sounded nothing at all like Andreas, Fabian, or Cassia. Instead, they sounded very much like the blood prince’s acolyte.

III

Andreas blinked, his vision adjusting to the strange, shifting light of the space around him. A gray-robed figure stood before him, his face pale but familiar.

"Decimus?" Andreas asked, uncertain.

The man nodded. "Yes, Andreas, it is I. But I don't know where we are."

Andreas's gaze swept their surroundings. Wherever this was, it wasn't the mortal world, nor was it the black meadow within his own mind. His skin, once sticky with the blood that had drenched him moments ago, was inexplicably clean. Not a single crimson stain remained. The space around them was in flux, dissolving and reforming in a maddening cycle.

One moment, they stood in the villa. In the next, the scene melted into a dense forest, the air thick with the scent of pine and damp earth. Then a wide plain stretched endlessly before them, the horizon ablaze with a red-tinged sky. Finally, they found themselves enclosed in the suffocating darkness of a cave, the only light a faint, flickering glow from unseen sources.

"We are in a transmuted space."

Andreas stiffened and turned. His breath caught as he came face-to-face with the demon who shared his soul and body. It had been some time since they last stood eye to eye, and the sight of Andras the Deathchaser was jarring.

He was not in his demonic form and his angelic wings were absent. Instead, Andras appeared as a man—a strikingly handsome one. His long dark hair framed sharp features, and his piercing eyes gleamed with intelligence.

The corner of Andras's lips tugged into a wry smile. "It's been a while, hasn't it, my boy?"

"What is this place? Are we trapped here?"

The demon sighed. "It seems so. This place isn't unlike the black meadow. Spiritual beings—angels, demons, and the like—can create such spaces when the need arises."

Andreas frowned. "So this place is...in-between?"

The Deathchaser nodded. "Precisely. Neither the mortal world nor the unseen realm. It's why you can see me in this form. It's also why Decimus is here, his spirit shielded from the watchful eyes of angels and demons alike." He glanced at Decimus with an arched brow. "Safe, in a manner of speaking."

"How do we escape from here?" Decimus asked, searching for any sign of an exit. "We need to rescue Cassia!"

Andras furrowed his brow. "I will try to find a weak point. There must be a way to break through. After all, Absalona did not want you dead, my boy."

That much was true. Absalona had spared his life for a reason—she wanted him for herself. To turn him into her next blood prince. But she lacked the strength to attempt it now. She needed more power. And when she had it, she would try again.

Questions burned in his mind. How long had Absalona possessed Cassia? Why Cassia of all people? Why not Valen, her loyal servant, directly? Was it because Cassia's faith had already fractured, leaving her vulnerable to Absalona's dark influence?

They hadn't the luxury of time to sit and ponder. Time was slipping away, and every moment brought

Absalona closer to the village. Closer to freeing the Blood Militia. Closer to enslaving the villagers in a blood sacrifice on a grand scale.

"We must hurry!" Decimus cried. "There is no telling what Absalona will do to Cassia!"

"Calm down, priest," Andras growled. "We are stuck here for the time being. Complaining about it won't make the process any faster."

"How might we assist you?" Andreas asked.

"By shutting your mouths and letting me concentrate."

Within moments, the ground beneath their feet rumbled and shook. The ever-shifting landscape quivered, growing even more unstable. Jagged fissures appeared in the ground, glowing faintly as if something beneath was struggling to break free.

"What is happening?" Decimus asked, wide-eyed.

"Have you done it, Andras?"

The demon shook his head, his expression grim. "This isn't my doing. Perhaps I misjudged. Perhaps this isn't quite like a transmuted space after all." His gaze darkened. "It feels more like the manipulations Valen was able to conjure."

Of course—his powers had originated from his maker, Absalona.

The landscape around them blurred, the colors bleeding together in a dizzying swirl. The ground disappeared, replaced with cold, hard stone. The hazy air gave way to the faint, flickering glow of candlelight.

And then the scene sharpened into focus. They stood inside a stone building, alight with dozens of candles. In the center of the room stood a gathering of people cloaked in deep red robes, their faces hidden beneath hoods.

"Where are we now?" Andreas asked. The space around them, at least, seemed stable.

"I know this place," Decimus said, his voice low, as he scanned the room. "This is the temple. But who are these people?"

Andras smirked. "Interesting," he drawled. "It would seem Absalona's power extends beyond mere space manipulation. She can twist time itself."

"Can they see us?" Andreas asked.

"It appears not," the Deathchaser said. "We are like apparitions here. Not unlike our dear Decimus." He glanced at the priest with a mocking smile.

"We are wasting time," Decimus snapped. "You must find a way out of this madness!"

Andras's eyes flared with a crimson light. "Silence, priest! Perhaps Absalona wants us to see this."

See what, exactly? The robed figures chanted in a language alien to Andreas. It was neither Greek, Latin, nor Aramaic. Something older, darker.

As the chanting grew louder, the group parted, dividing into two halves that stepped aside to reveal the centerpiece of their ritual: a stone altar, on which a naked young girl lay dead, a ceremonial dagger protruding from her chest. Rivulets of blood spilled down the grooves of the stone, pooling at its base.

A sacrifice.

Decimus gasped, staggering back as though struck. "This is an abomination!"

"Recall that this temple is where you chose to establish your church," the Deathchaser said. There was a glint of wicked pleasure in his crimson eyes, as if he relished the spectacle of blood sacrifices. "Imagine the sheer number of sacrificial deaths that have stained these stones over the years."

"We must stop this!" Decimus said through gritted teeth.

"This is only a memory," Andreas said. "Whatever we are witnessing here has already come to pass."

Andras nodded. "Indeed. So sit back and enjoy the spectacle, priest."

A man stepped forward and tugged free the sacrificial dagger from the young girl. He raised it to his lips and licked the blood dripping from the dagger's blade. His eyes shut as if savoring the taste.

Decimus turned away in disgust.

"Any luck, Andras?" Andreas asked, creeping tightness settling over him.

"I'm trying, my boy," Andras said. "As much as I enjoy this rare opportunity to converse face-to-face, I care little for being imprisoned in someone else's twisted, manipulated space."

A thunderous banging sounded. The followers of Absalona froze, their chanting silenced as they turned toward the wooden gate at the far end of the temple.

"What was that?" Decimus asked.

Another booming crash echoed. The heavy wood groaned under the assault, the iron hinges straining.

Andreas reached for his sword, but the Deathchaser stayed his hand. "I wouldn't, my boy. Besides, it will do you no good. We are merely spectators here."

The gate splintered under the next strike, shards of wood flying as the barrier gave way. Roman soldiers, gladii in hand, stormed into the temple.

The slaughter was swift and brutal. Throats were cut, limbs severed. Blades pierced stomachs and hearts, leaving behind crumpled bodies that sprawled lifeless on the blood-soaked floor.

Decimus looked on with horror in his eyes. "Can we do nothing to stop this?"

Andras shrugged nonchalantly. "You could try, priest, but it will avail you nothing."

"This would explain," Andreas said, "why Absalona seeks vengeance against Rome."

Decimus trembled. "It is a massacre!"

Blood sprayed in every direction.

"You have to hand it to the Romans," the Deathchaser said with some admiration. "They are efficient killers."

Something caught Andreas's attention—a strange spiritual being hovering above.

"Look."

Was it Absalona? It must be. Like her followers, she, too, wore a red robe, but one embroidered with intricate patterns. The robe flowed as though it were made of rivers of blood. The red robe went with the tears she shed, for they, too, were red as blood.

"She's...crying?" Decimus said.

"Her followers are dying," Andreas said grimly. "A demon like Absalona needs worship to sustain her power. Without them, she weakens."

Her cries tore through the sound of all the killing.

The Deathchaser grunted, unimpressed. "You'd think all this blood would please her."

Andreas shook his head. "It is likely the blood sacrifices were not among her followers."

The battle below raged on, a frenzy of Roman efficiency as soldiers cut down every robed figure in their path. None were spared. But amidst the slaughter, one of Absalona's followers, a man with a blood-streaked face and terror in his eyes, pushed a young boy forward, shielding him with his body.

"Go! Run!" the man shouted.

The boy, no older than twelve, hesitated for only a heartbeat. His wide, tear-filled eyes locked with the man's before he turned and bolted, his small frame darting through the chaos. He leapt through one of the temple's window openings and disappeared into the night.

"Well, now," the Deathchaser said. "It seems someone did manage to escape. Likely the ancestor of the Blood Militia."

He was the only survivor. The soldiers had left no one else standing. The temple floor was littered with the bodies of Absalona's followers.

Decimus made the sign of the cross. "That poor boy. He was all alone."

"Don't feel too sorry for him, my dear Decimus," Andras said. "That boy not only survived—he rebuilt the followers of Absalona. Because of him, you are dead, and your daughter's life hangs by a thread."

Decimus recoiled as if struck, guilt and anger contorting his countenance.

"We must hurry, Andras," Andreas said. "More lives are at stake."

Andras nodded. "I've almost got it."

The Deathchaser had been working tirelessly, channeling his dark aether, probing the boundaries of the manipulated space for any sign of weakness. His efforts, subtle and unseen, had been constant even as they bore witness to the horrors unfolding around them.

But then the Deathchaser's expression darkened. "Damn!"

"What?" Decimus asked.

Before anyone could answer, the temple began to shift. The solid stone walls wavered and melted. The bloodstained floor darkened, the crimson liquid transforming into a slick, black sludge that oozed and bubbled. The oppressive darkness of night gave way to a sudden, blinding burst of light as morning broke through the illusion.

"Brace yourselves," Andreas called out. "The space is changing once more."

Andreas steeled himself, ready for whatever might come next.

IV

The Blood Militia had gathered in the village's agora. A tense silence hung in the air, thick and suffocating. The villagers, hesitant but curious, crowded around the spectacle, their whispers hushed but urgent.

Who had freed them? And why?

Marcia stood near the edge of the crowd, her heart pounding. Among the Blood Militia was a figure she recognized.

"Mirko," she murmured under her breath.

He had been missing since Andreas's confrontation with the vampires Agrippa and Dosia. He had slipped away unnoticed while the others fought. And now here he was, standing before them. Worse still, it was clear he had not returned alone. He had released the rest of his cohort.

"Do you remember him?" Marcia asked Agrippa and Dosia.

"Yes," Agrippa answered, his jaw set. "He's the leader of the Blood Militia. He brought them here months ago, bent on forcing conversions to worship some goddess of theirs." He struggled to remember. "I believe her name was Absalona."

Marcia frowned. "Absalona?"

"The temple Decimus took over," Dosia explained. "It was originally devoted to her."

Marcia's stomach twisted at the revelation. "But where is this Absalona? Is she a demon?"

Agrippa nodded. "Very likely she is. We never saw her—not once. Neither, as far as we know, did Valen."

The name hung in the air like a dark omen. Absalona. It was the first time Marcia had heard it spoken aloud, and the sound of it sent an uneasy shiver down her spine. Whoever this demon was, she had been a shadowy figure. Perhaps forgotten for many years.

Mirko thrust his fist into the air. "Hear me!" his voice boomed. "A great reckoning will befall this village and its people unless you turn away from your evil ways and give your blood to the blood prince!"

The crowd stirred uneasily, murmurs rippling through the villagers like the first gusts of a coming tempest. Fear and confusion painted their faces, and no one dared to step forward.

"He doesn't know that Valen has been slain," Dosia whispered as she leaned toward Marcia.

"No," Marcia whispered back, her voice tight. She darted nervous glances around her. Where was the demon slayer? He had to hurry.

Absalona. The name gnawed at her.

Cassia. What if Absalona had possessed her? It explained so much—the strange behavior, the sudden changes. If it were true, then this was far from over.

The villagers' voices swelled, restless and unruly. The crowd shifted, uneasy. And then someone noticed Agrippa and Dosia.

"Aren't you with them?" the villager shouted.

Heads turned. One by one, more villagers looked at them, their expressions shifting from curiosity to anger. Suspicion spread across the agora.

"You were!" another shouted. "You were the vampires!"

Concern clouded Dosia. She gripped Agrippa's hand tightly.

"We are man and woman again," Agrippa said. "Can't you see that?"

The evidence was plain to anyone to see; they no longer bore the deathly pallor of vampires nor the deadly fangs. And they were standing under the bright light of day, unharmed. If they were still creatures of the night, the sun's merciless rays would have turned them to ash by now.

But reason had fled the villagers.

"You took my son from me!" a woman screamed. Her words struck like a whip.

The villagers' eyes burned with a singular, dangerous intent.

Revenge.

Marcia stepped forward. At least they knew she wasn't a vampire. Perhaps they would listen to her.

"It's true," she said, her voice carrying over the restless crowd. "They were creatures of the night. But they were as much victims as you and your families."

Her words hung in the air for a moment, and for a fleeting second, she thought she saw some hesitation in their eyes. But the villagers weren't ready to relent.

"Yet they still live!"

"They live because they were saved!" Marcia countered. "Saved by the demon slayer Andreas."

"What's this about the demon slayer?"

The villagers fell silent and parted, revealing Mirko. He came towards them, scowling. Two members of the Blood Militia flanked him.

"I remember you, girl," Mirko said to Marcia. "You were the one who summoned for the demon slayer, weren't you?"

Marcia held her ground, though her heart pounded against her ribs. She refused to let him see her fear.

Mirko's scowl deepened, his voice like acid. "Know this, girl: your demon slayer surely lies dead at the hands of the blood prince."

Before Marcia could respond, Agrippa stepped forward. Whether it was courage or recklessness driving him, Marcia couldn't be sure.

"I would not be so certain of that, Mirko," Agrippa said.

Mirko's mouth fell open, face blanched. Even the two Blood Militia members at his side exchanged quizzical looks.

"Agrippa? And Dosia?" Mirko stammered. "Your vampirism is reversed. How is this possible?"

"We were freed from Valen's curse," Agrippa said. He squared his shoulders. "We are man and woman again. Children of God."

Mirko's gaze darted between them. "But that could only mean—"

"Valen is slain," Marcia said. "Your blood prince is no more. Andreas was victorious, and he will bring back Fabian and Cassia."

Mirko's composure cracked. "No...no..." he muttered. "We were to take over Rome. Absalona would rule over the Empire."

"Like your blood prince," Agrippa said, "those aspirations of yours are finished. Now leave this village in peace—you and your so-called Blood Militia."

Mirko shook with barely restrained rage. The villagers, emboldened by the absence of the vampires' threat, began shouting in defiance.

"Leave our village!"

"Get out!"

The Blood Militia shifted uneasily, their confidence faltering under the villagers' growing rebellion.

Marcia's attention, however, was drawn elsewhere. Out of the corner of her eye, she spotted a figure in the distance, walking toward them. A girl, her blond hair flowing in the breeze.

"It's Cassia!" Marcia exclaimed.

As the girl drew closer, there was no doubt—it was Cassia. Her familiar features came into focus. Relief surged through Marcia, but it was fleeting.

Something was wrong.

"Where is Fabian?" Dosia's brow furrowed as she scanned the horizon. "And the demon slayer?"

Had Cassia escaped on her own? Was that even possible? A shadow passed over Marcia. She instinctively took a step back, as though trying to distance herself from the girl she had called her friend.

Something about Cassia was...off. Her movements, her posture—it was too calm, too poised. And her eyes, though still the same striking blue, seemed to hold a darkness that hadn't been there before.

What had happened to Andreas and Fabian?

Oh, God. Could it be?

Mirko's expression transformed as Cassia approached. His rage faded, replaced not with defeat but with rapturous joy.

"It's you, isn't it?" he said. "I knew it. I knew it that day I first saw you."

Mirko fell to his knees before Cassia, his eyes brimming with tears. But his veneration wasn't for Cassia as Marcia knew her—it was for someone else entirely.

"You are her," Mirko whispered, voice thick with awe.

"Cassia," Agrippa said, "she seems different."

Dosia hugged herself, her face pale. "I feel it, too. Like my very blood grows cold."

Marcia shook her head in disbelief. "No, no, no," she whispered under her breath. "Please, God, no!"

Mirko prostrated himself before Cassia, pressing his forehead to the ground. Then he looked up, his face a mask of adoration. Tears streaked his cheeks, but they were the tears of a man who believed he was witnessing a divine revelation.

"My queen," he said. "My goddess. My everything. You are Absalona."

Cassia was no longer herself. The girl Marcia had known was gone, her body now a vessel for something far darker.

Absalona had returned.

V

A bustling city surrounded Decimus.

Merchants peddled wares of every kind—freshly baked bread, glinting trinkets, bolts of colorful fabric. A soft breeze brought the mingling scents of spices, sweat, and the nearby sea.

Andras wrinkled his nose. "I can smell the filth of you mortals."

Andreas looked around him. "This is Iader."

"Yes, it is," Decimus said. Wonder seized him. This wasn't just any version of Iader; it was the Iader of his past. The city of his youth.

He left Andreas and Andras and started toward the city's agora. Once there, he surveyed the area.

And then he saw it.

"There!"

Andreas and Andras caught up to him.

"What's wrong?" Andreas asked.

Decimus didn't answer immediately. His gaze was fixed on the figures before him. Finally, he said, "That's me."

Himself as a boy. He wore a plain, ragged tunic. His greasy, unwashed hair clung to his face, and his skin was dark from the sun.

"And that's my mother and father."

His father stood rigid, disapproval clear on his face. His mother, glaring, dragged the boy by the arm, her mouth moving in silent reprimand.

Had he done something wrong? The answer was as inevitable as the rising sun. Of course he had. What a stupid question.

He could do nothing right. That was how they made him feel. Every harsh word, every sharp glare, every blow—they were etched into his memory like scars on flesh. The sun wasn't the only thing that darkened his skin. The bruises told their own story, one of pain and humiliation.

And yet, as he looked at his parents now, he felt...nothing. They were strangers to him. Whatever love he might have once felt for them had long since withered.

"They did not love me," he confessed. "And I, in turn, did not love them. Even though I should honor them as it is written in the Holy Scriptures. When I returned to Iader as a man, I was glad to learn they had both died. No children came after me. The line ended with them."

"That woman trailing behind you," Andreas said.

Oh, yes. She was there, too. The sight of her made his chest tighten with an emotion he couldn't quite name. She had been his only friend, his only solace in those dark days.

He made the sign of the cross. "That's the Theotokos."

She wore a robe of deep crimson, the fabric flowing around her. She followed behind the boy—his younger self—her steps light and soundless, her presence otherworldly. Though Decimus could see her as clearly as the sun above, no one else seemed to notice her.

She had come to him in his dreams. She had been with him in his waking life when the weight of his parents' contempt crushed his spirit. If not for her quiet, unwavering presence, he would have despaired completely. She was the tether that kept him from slipping into darkness.

She was beautiful—achingly so. Her features possessed a quiet elegance, each detail drawing the eye effortlessly.

The Deathchaser grunted. "I hate to be the bearer of bad tidings, my dear Decimus, but that is no Theotokos."

Decimus furrowed his brow. "No, it must be. She told me she was."

But had she? No—she had never actually revealed her name. She had never claimed to be the Theotokos. She had simply been there, a source of comfort.

It was only after he met Pamphilus and Efrem and heard their stories of Jesus that the idea had taken root. It was he who had convinced himself that she was the Theotokos.

But if she wasn't the Mother of God, then who was she?

"That's the same woman we saw in the temple," Andreas said. "The one lamenting the murder of her followers. That is Absalona."

Decimus shook his head. "It can't be."

"How long had she been following you?" Andreas asked.

"For as long as I can remember. Though I could not always see her. But why would she choose me?"

At that moment, the young Decimus stumbled and fell. His knees scraped against the rough, dusty ground, the skin breaking open. He winced but didn't cry out, his small hands trembling as he tried to push himself up.

Then his father stormed toward him. Without a word, the man snatched the boy's arm, yanking him to his feet. The boy's knees buckled, but he steadied himself quickly, biting his lip to stifle the tears welling in his eyes. He knew better than to cry; tears only invited more punishment.

"You were an abused and neglected child," the Deathchaser said, his voice cold and matter-of-fact. "Such children are easy to manipulate. They are impressionable and eager to accept the comfort a so-called divine being offers them."

Decimus flinched. "But I did not feel possessed. And Absalona does not possess me now."

Andreas knit his brow. "Perhaps someone intervened," he offered. "Someone who saved you."

The air around them seemed to vibrate, and the world became a blur of motion. Time itself accelerated, and the people around them transformed into streaks of color, their movements too fast to follow. The sun rose and set in rapid succession, day and night cycling like the turning of a great wheel.

Then, as suddenly as it began, the frenzy stopped. The world slowed, and time resumed its natural rhythm. They now stood in a different scene: a young Decimus sat cross-legged on the ground, his face brighter, his expression softer. He listened intently to two men, both clad in simple robes, their voices calm and measured as they spoke.

"Who are they?" Andreas asked.

"Pamphilus and Efrem. They were traveling priests, spreading the Gospel. I left my parents, my home, and joined them."

The red-robed woman, whose presence Decimus could no longer deny, was indeed Absalona. But now, she was nowhere to be seen. Had Pamphilus and Efrem kept her at bay all those years ago? Had their faith shielded the young Decimus from her grasp?

He remembered how he had told them, in his innocence, that he had seen the Theotokos. Did they somehow know it wasn't her he had seen but a demon cloaked in comforting deceit? If so, they had saved him in more ways than one; not just from his despair but from the clutches of an evil spiritual being who would have consumed him entirely.

Time accelerated again in a dizzying rush. The world blurred around them, faster and faster, the days blinking by. The warmth of summer gave way to the chill of autumn, which in turn dissolved into the frost of winter, only for the blooms of spring to emerge moments later. The cycle repeated until it all suddenly stopped.

When the world stilled, Decimus found himself standing before another version of himself: no longer a boy, but a young man. He held the hand of a woman whose belly was round with child.

The memories flooded back to him with startling clarity. "But then I returned to Iader," he said. "That was where I met Lavinia, my wife. We were married, and soon after, her belly swelled with our child. Cassia."

The young man looked at Lavinia with tenderness and love. Her eyes sparkled, and she smiled up at him, her hands resting gently on her pregnant belly.

But the warmth of the scene chilled abruptly as a shadow stirred at the edge of the sunlight. It slithered forward, taking form.

It was Absalona, her figure deformed and unsettling. Her skin was a sickly gray, stretched tightly over her sharp cheekbones as though she had been starved. Her sunken eyes glowed faintly, red as dying embers. Yet, despite her ghastly appearance, she smiled.

"It seems," the Deathchaser said, "that despite the passage of time, Absalona did not forget you."

"Had she been waiting for me? Expecting me to return?"

"It is difficult to possess a priest," Andreas answered. "But not impossible. I've seen it done before."

Absalona glided through the air. She descended toward Lavinia, coiling herself around Lavinia like a serpent.

Her bony fingers stroked Lavinia's blond hair with a mockery of affection, whispering into her ear. Lavinia, radiant in her joy and oblivious to the demonic presence entwined around her, continued to smile at her husband.

And the Decimus of that time smiled back at her, blissfully ignorant of the malevolence lurking so close. Absalona had not revealed herself to him as she had in his childhood.

"She couldn't possess me," Decimus said. "So she chose Lavinia instead."

"What happened to your wife?" Andreas asked.

"She died in childbirth."

"Then it was not Lavinia she possessed, but Cassia." Andreas turned to his demon. "Is it possible for a demon to possess a baby?"

Andras cocked an eyebrow. "Have you ever spent time with an infant? My boy, they're little demons themselves! All that crying and whining—it's enough to drive even the most patient saint mad."

Andreas shot him a dark look and Andras sighed dramatically, his smirk fading as he straightened. "But no," he admitted. "There would be no purpose in possessing a baby. Besides, your God protects them—all of them. Every single one."

"Then she waited," Andreas said. "Waited until Cassia could accept her into her heart."

"But Cassia wouldn't do that," Decimus said. "She was a follower of Christ. She was baptized."

The Deathchaser shrugged. "No use debating the matter, my dear Decimus. We saw the truth of it with our own eyes."

Without warning, the city vanished. Blackness swallowed everything around them.

"Andras, are you close to finding a way out of here?"

The demon didn't answer immediately. His arms remained crossed over his chest. From time to time, his muscles tensed, the faintest flicker of strain crossing his face. Whatever he was doing, it required focus. And effort.

Then, a voice pierced the silence.

"Papa! Papa, please help! Help me!"

Cassia!

Decimus turned, and there she was: his little girl, eyes wide with fear, huddled in her bed, surrounded by the familiar walls of their home in Iader.

Absalona loomed above her.

Decimus cried, "Cassia!" His words echoed in the emptiness, but they seemed powerless, lost in the chasm of space between them.

"Enough, girl!" Absalona hissed, baring her fangs fully as she moved closer to the trembling child. "You are mine!"

"Nooooo!" Decimus's scream tore from his throat. He stretched out his hand toward Cassia.

Her tear-streaked face turned toward him, her small hand reaching out.

And then they vanished like smoke.

In their place was the black meadow.

***

Andreas stood on the second-floor balcony, gazing out at the Adriatic Sea shimmering in the mid-afternoon sun. The villa was empty—no sign of Absalona, Andras, or Decimus. He had returned to the mortal world, with the remnants of Absalona's twisted space now reduced to a circle of dried blood around him.

You did it, Andras.

The demon's voice echoed in his mind. *"Indeed, my boy. But the priest is displeased."*

Decimus's voice cracked. *"I...I must save her!"*

Andreas's chest tightened as a sudden chill swept over him. His legs buckled, and he fell to one knee, his muscles locking, his teeth clenched against the overwhelming force wrenching itself from deep within him.

Then, as abruptly as it began, the feeling vanished. He exhaled sharply, sweat beading on his brow.

Before him stood the ghost of Decimus.

"Decimus? It's not safe for you out here."

Doubtless, scavenger demons would sense Decimus's vulnerable spirit and begin rallying to claim him.

"I am sorry, Andreas," Decimus said, desperation in his voice. "But I must go and rescue Cassia. I am faster as a ghost. Perhaps I can intercept Absalona before she hurts Cassia—or anyone else."

Andreas rose. "We can do this together."

Decimus shook his head, his spectral form flickering faintly. "We have already wasted so much time."

"The scavenger demons will come for you, Decimus. If I am not there, you will have no defense against them."

Decimus smiled bittersweetly. "I know, Andreas. But I must try."

"Let the poor bastard go, my boy. Hades awaits his damned soul."

Decimus sailed over the balcony, his melancholic eyes watching Andreas, his hands clasped in front of him in prayer. "Thank you for getting me this far, Andreas. May God be with me."

Before Andreas could respond, Decimus swept through the air, heading toward the village.

The distant waves of the sea crashed against the shore. Andreas gripped the hilt of his sword as he whispered to himself, "May God be with us both."

VI

"Yes, Mirko, it is I."

She had Cassia's face, but her posture was different—rigid, commanding—and her voice carried none of Cassia's warmth.

This was not Cassia. This was not the friend Marcia loved.

"You have been a faithful servant, Mirko," she said, her tone even, almost dispassionate.

Mirko, on his hands and knees with his head bowed, said, "I have devoted my life to you as my forefathers did."

Cassia—or the thing wearing her form—lowered herself gracefully to her knees. She placed her hands gently under Mirko's arms and lifted him to his feet.

"Then come," she said. "Receive your reward, servant."

She pulled him into an embrace. Mirko clung to her, desperate and childlike, his fingers clutching at her robe as though he were holding on to his mother.

"How I have waited for this moment," he whispered.

She gave a cold, empty smile before parting her lips to reveal sharp, elongated fangs. In one swift motion, she sank them into Mirko's neck.

A guttural gasp escaped his lips as his body went rigid in her arms. She held him there, her grip tightening, and began to drink. The sound of it was wet and savage. Mirko's hands twitched, then fell limp at his sides as his life drained away.

Screams erupted from the villagers. Panic swept through them as they scattered in every direction.

Even among the Blood Militia, there was hesitation. A few exchanged uncertain glances, their hands hovering near their weapons. Some slowly drew their clubs, their expressions unsure.

Cassia—or was it Absalona now?—threw her head back, retracting her fangs from Mirko's neck. His ashen face tilted unnaturally as she released him. The body crumpled to the ground, twitched once, then fell still.

Absalona turned her gaze toward the remaining Blood Militia, Mirko's blood smeared across her mouth and chin. "You are the Blood Militia, are you not?"

One of them, voice trembling but resolute, muttered an assent to her question.

"You have served well," Absalona said, nodding, "but I require blood."

She slashed her hand across, and a crimson arc tore through them.

Marcia flinched at the sickening sound of throats being severed in unison. The Blood Militia staggered, clutching at their necks as blood erupted in fountains. Their bodies collapsed one by one, lifeless, into a growing sea of red.

Absalona opened her mouth and drew in a deep, rattling breath. The pools of blood slithered across the ground, coalescing into streams that rushed toward her. The liquid lifted into the air and disappeared into her open mouth. Her throat moved rhythmically as she swallowed, consuming every last drop until not even a stain remained.

When it was done, she sighed with satisfaction. "Perfect." She licked the last trace of blood from her lips. "But I still need more."

"Come, Marcia!" Agrippa said, tugging at her arm. "We must flee!"

But Marcia resisted, shaking off his grip. Her heart pounded, every instinct screaming at her to run, but she couldn't. She couldn't leave. Her feet moved as if of their own accord, carrying her forward, closer to the demon wearing her friend's face.

"Cassia, are you still in there?"

Absalona turned her fiery gaze toward Marcia. "Ah, the traitor. How brave of you to show yourself to me."

Marcia took a steady breath, firming her resolve. She clutched the small wooden cross around her neck. She would not let fear take hold. Her trust in the Lord was her shield, and it gave her strength to stand before this monster.

"Where is Fabian? And Andreas?" she demanded.

"Fabian lies dead."

Her words burned through Marcia's heart like acid.

"As for your demon slayer," Absalona continued, "I will deal with him later."

Which meant Andreas was alive. If Absalona hadn't killed him, what had she done? Was he injured? Imprisoned?

"What did you do with Cassia?"

"She called to me," Absalona said, "and I answered her call. She is with me now."

"You lie, demon!" Marcia snapped with defiance.

Absalona glared. "A demon?" she hissed. "I am no demon, girl!" She raised her chin. "I am a goddess! And I will prove to the world what I am capable of—once I've had my fill of blood." Her eyes trained on Marcia like a prowler to its prey. "Perhaps you should be my next victim."

"Marcia, please!" Dosia's voice cracked with urgency. "We must go!"

Marcia shook her head. "No. I do not fear you, demon."

But the tremor in her voice betrayed her.

"Stupid girl!" Absalona spat. "I should have rid myself of you long ago!"

Marcia closed her eyes, hands enclosing the cross around her neck. "Even though I walk through the darkest valley, I will fear no evil, for You, Lord, are with me; Your rod and Your staff, they comfort me."

She heard the steady thud of Absalona's footsteps drawing nearer.

"I will savor your blood. I will enjoy every last drop."

Absalona lunged, seizing Marcia by the throat. Marcia's eyes flew open as she was lifted off the ground, her feet dangling helplessly.

Marcia gasped for breath, her lungs straining as the demon's iron grip crushed her throat, teetering on the edge of snapping her neck.

Her prayers fell silent.

"Stop! Leave her be, Absalona!"

That voice—

Decimus.

VII

Absalona released her grip, and Marcia dropped to the ground. She gasped and coughed violently, her hands clutching at her throat as precious air rushed back into her lungs.

Decimus had arrived just in time, though it appeared Absalona had taken her Blood Militia as a blood sacrifice. Decimus mourned for them. Though their end was tragic, it had been one of their own making.

"You. The priest. But you should be dead."

It tore at his heart to see his daughter speak and act so monstrously. Was she powerless against the demon? No doubt she was. But now he was here, and he would save her, no matter the cost.

"Indeed, I am dead," Decimus said. "But I will not leave this world until I know my daughter—and my family"—his gaze swept over Marcia, Agrippa, and Dosia—"are safe. I failed Fabian, but I will not fail the others."

"Father!" Marcia said as she crawled away from Absalona. The demon paid her no mind, her attention fixed on Decimus.

"Everything's going to be all right now, Marcia," Decimus said. "Trust in the Lord."

Dosia helped Marcia to her feet as Agrippa said, "Decimus? Is it really you?"

Decimus gave a solemn nod. "It is. And it is good to see you both returned to yourselves again. Please, take Marcia and go."

"We will stay here with you," Marcia said despite the fear in her eyes. "We will help you in any way we can."

Such courage, such faith; he couldn't help but admire Marcia. In such a short time, she had grown into an extraordinary woman.

"I cannot allow any of you to suffer further for my sins," Decimus said. "Find somewhere safe to hide and then pray—with all your heart, mind, and soul. Leave this to me."

As they turned to flee, the air seemed to crackle with energy, and a voice like thunder stopped them in their tracks.

"You are not going anywhere!"

Absalona lunged, swift and deadly, but Decimus surged forward, his ghostly form slipping effortlessly through her. She stopped, recoiling from the unexpected sensation. A sharp hiss escaped her lips, and she cursed vehemently, leaping back and glaring at Decimus.

The instant Decimus passed through her, he felt a darkness as vile as the Deathchaser's.

How could he stop her alone? Andreas was still some distance away. Could he stall her long enough? Or was there another way?

"Go!" he shouted to the others.

They resumed their escape, but Marcia looked back at him.

"Fear not, Marcia. Andreas is coming."

Absalona's smile returned as she lifted her hands, and as she did so the ground responded, shifting and rising. The earth groaned as massive walls sprung up, higher and higher until they loomed over the group like the walls of a fortress. The jagged stone stretched too high to scale, their escape sealed off.

"As I said," Absalona purred, "none of you are leaving."

Decimus glided forward, positioning himself between Absalona and the others.

"They will leave here alive," he said. "And you will release my daughter from your possession."

Absalona's lips curled into a sinister smile. "She is mine, priest. She wanted me."

"You forced yourself on her," Decimus shot back. "She did not want this."

"She wanted me. She needed me. She called out for me."

"Why?" Marcia said. "What would she want with a demon? She had her father. She had me, and the rest of the church."

Absalona's gaze snapped to Marcia. "But did she? The girl was lonely. She cried out for help, but her cries fell on deaf ears. Her mother taken from her. Moved to a new place. A father who ignored her. A friend who only cared for her father's attention."

"That's not true!" Marcia denied it, but even Decimus could see the truth in Absalona's words. "I love Cassia."

Absalona shook her head. "No. You loved her father. You loved the church he was building. You wanted so desperately to be part of it all. And in that blind ambition, you used Cassia as nothing more than a stepping stone to get what you wanted."

Marcia's gaze fell to the ground, her face flushed with shame. "No...that's not true..."

"Is it not?"

"Do not be led astray, Marcia," Decimus said. "Demons lie."

"And what of you, priest?" she hissed. "You ignored your own daughter. All for the sake of your god."

"You cannot fool me, Absalona. I was always there for her. I would do anything for her."

Absalona cocked an eyebrow. "Including murder?"

Of course, she knew. She had witnessed it herself through Cassia's eyes. Decimus's jaw tightened, but he said nothing.

"Father?" Marcia's voice was small, uncertain. "What is she saying?"

He had told them it was an accident. That Valen had slipped and fallen. That there was nothing he nor Cassia could have done to save him.

"Oh, you withheld the truth from your flock?" Absalona gave a throaty chuckle. "I am not the least bit surprised. 'You shall not murder'—is that not one of your god's commandments?"

"What is she talking about, Decimus?" Agrippa said.

"Valen," Absalona said, her voice almost pitying. "Dear, dear Valen. You killed him."

"You said it was an accident," Marcia said. Her wide eyes searched Decimus's face, desperate to cling to the version of him she had always believed in.

"And it was," Decimus was quick to answer. "I never meant to hurt him."

Absalona tsked as though chastising a child. "More lies, Decimus? Is that why the demons are coming for your soul, and not a single angel has descended to guide you to Paradise? Have you not repented of your grave sin?"

Decimus grimaced. He could not hide from what he had done to Valen, nor the passion he had felt while doing it, or his refusal to follow the Lord's call to repentance. There was no point in hiding anymore. He could not run from it any longer.

"My sin is indeed grave, and I did not repent it. I wanted Valen to die for what he did to my daughter."

He glanced at the others but their eyes didn't meet his. He had failed them, betrayed their trust, and hurt them in more ways than one. All of this was his fault, and he had to make it right.

"But now I see," he continued, his voice gaining a quiet strength. "He was just a part of your plan. You orchestrated all of it."

"Valen's death was your doing, not mine. I intended to take your body."

Decimus placed a hand on his chest, his translucent form flickering. "Why? Why me? You were there when I was a child. I remember you now—the woman in the red robe."

Absalona's expression darkened. "Because of your brokenness. In you, I saw myself—a boy growing to hate the world around him, just as I hated the world the day Rome nearly wiped out my followers."

"It's true," he admitted. "I did hate the world. I wished I had never been born. But that was before I found the Lord. He saved me. He showed me there was more than hate, more than suffering."

Absalona's face contorted as if she were about to be sick. "He did. But then you came back to me. And here you are. I always knew you would come back to me."

"Let Cassia go. And the others, too. Let my family live."

Absalona tilted her head, her gaze curious.

"Take..." Decimus faltered, glancing down at his translucent body. For a moment, uncertainty gnawed at him. But then he looked up, meeting Absalona's eyes with a hard, unwavering stare. The determination in his voice was unshakable as he said, "Take me in their stead."

VIII

"My boy, you don't honestly think this is worth it, do you?" the Deathchaser's voice slithered into Andreas's mind.

"I can't let Decimus fall into the hands of the demon scavengers."

As soon as Decimus set off alone, Andreas hurried back to the village. Thank God his horse was still tethered where he'd left it. He mounted quickly, urging the animal forward at full speed.

There was no telling what Absalona might do. She could drain the villagers dry or enslave them all as her vampires. And with Decimus on his own, the priestly ghost stood little chance of stopping her.

"Let the scavengers have his soul. Decimus is a murderer. A sinner. Worst of all, he is unrepentant. Such souls are meant for damnation."

Andreas tightened his grip on the reins. "Perhaps I can save him."

The Deathchaser sighed. *"The duty of a demon slayer, I suppose. But what you really need, my boy, is rest."*

He wasn't wrong. Weakened and wounded, Andreas could feel his body protesting with every stride of the horse. He'd managed to stop the bleeding by tearing strips from his cloak to bandage his injuries, but they were temporary measures at best. His muscles ached and his head swam with fatigue.

He would recover on the ride. His strength would return in time. For now, he couldn't afford to think about his own suffering. There were lives at stake.

"Plenty of time for rest after I've slain Absalona."

Andreas drove the horse onward, his legs gripping its sides as he urged it to run faster.

"My heart breaks for the horse," Andras muttered. *"You'll run her to an early grave."*

Andreas ignored him, his focus fixed on the road ahead. "Now that we know Absalona is behind this, do you remember who she is?"

"Not at all, my boy. As I said, she was likely a child born from the relations of a woman and a Son of God. She is not a god or even a true demon—she is a nephil."

The nephilim. The Holy Scriptures spoke of them from the time of Noah. Born of the wickedness between the daughters of man and the rebellious Sons of God known as the Watchers. The Watchers were meant to guide mortal men and women in a life of service to the Lord and to each other, but instead, they betrayed their duty, seducing and abusing the women, teaching all mortals forbidden knowledge to inflame their passions. The nephilim, born of these unions, carried the energy of divine beings—giants, titans, men and women of renown. They saw themselves as gods and rulers of the earth, boasting of their greatness.

"Then how did she become like this?"

"Nephilim are indeed powerful beings, but they take after their mortal mothers in one crucial way—they are mortal themselves. When a nephil dies, her soul neither ascends to Paradise nor descends to Hades."

"Then the soul roams the earth."

"Exactly, my boy. The soul of a nephil remains here, tethered to this realm, to haunt the people of God. They are not unlike wraiths—or even ghosts, like our dear Decimus. But with one terrifying difference: a nephil's

soul can possess a mortal body. Indeed, most of the demons your Christ exorcised were once nephilim. You must remember—even if the great Flood wiped out most of the nephilim, their souls persisted, wandering the earth."

"What other abilities do they wield?"

"Oh, all sorts!" Andras said with a hint of dark amusement. *"Though they lack the ability to call upon a Circle of Hades."*

At least there was that, though it offered little comfort. Absalona had already demonstrated her power to manipulate space in ways similar to a Circle of Hades. She could likely do everything the vampires could, too: hide in shadows, summon perpetual night, double her strength by feasting on blood, and who knew what else.

This battle would not be easily won.

"The real question, my boy, is what does Decimus hope to achieve?"

Andreas frowned. "I've been wondering that myself. It's clear that Absalona wants—and needs—power."

"Indeed. And her aether grows with the consumption of blood. The more blood she drinks, the greater her power."

"But she wants Decimus for something. Perhaps even more so now that he is a ghost. Can she...possess his ghost?"

"That would be impossible. It is more likely that she will absorb him, consume him as she consumes blood."

"What would she gain from that?"

"Have you not noticed, my boy?" Andras's voice took on a patronizing tone. *"Decimus is a man of God. He devoted his life to the Lord. If he had repented of Valen's murder, he would be in Paradise at this very moment. It is why the demon scavengers want him—and why, I suspect, Absalona desires him even more now."*

"They see the light of God in him," Andreas murmured, the realization settling over him like a cold weight.

Though everyone was made in God's image and carried His light within, only a rare few let that light shine brightly enough to draw the attention of spiritual beings. Decimus, despite his flaws and sins, was one of those rare souls. The light within him had not been extinguished, even in death.

"And they want that light for themselves. To pervert it, ruin it, corrupt it. It will grant her power beyond her imagining."

Andreas's fists clenched the reins tightly, his knuckles turning white. "Then we must hurry."

"Indeed—for the scavengers come."

Dark, menacing clouds gathered in the sky, a crimson glow flickering behind their dense cover.

A piercing screech split the air. Andreas glanced upward.

Scavenger demons swooped above, their skeletal forms barely held together by sickly skin. Their bony wings flapped in a stuttering rhythm, sending gusts of foul wind in their wake.

And they were heading straight for the village. Straight for Decimus.

Andreas kicked his horse forward, urgency driving them. Time was slipping away.

Hold on, Decimus, he thought grimly. *We're coming.*

IX

Absalona cocked her head. "You would make a deal with the devil?"

"You can have my soul," Decimus said, "but let my family go and release my daughter from your possession."

"No, Father!" Marcia cried. "Please, reconsider!"

Decimus turned to her, his gaze softening as he regarded Marcia and the others. He raised a hand as if to bless them, though it trembled with the weight of his confession.

"I must, my child. This evil is all my fault. I was so consumed by my church, so focused on building something I thought was for God, that I lost sight of the very values of our Lord and Savior. Values I had wished to imitate and instill in all of you.

"No longer did I seek humility. My life was not in service to those in need but in service to my own status. I let my pride guide me, not Christ. And for that, I failed you all. If I can save you now, I will gladly give myself to the whim of demons. None of you should suffer for the evil I wrought."

He faced Absalona now, who inhabited the body of his daughter, Cassia. He looked into her eyes—those same eyes he'd seen light up with laughter, now darkened with malice not her own. Could Cassia see him? Could she hear him through the suffocating control of the demon? His heart ached with the weight of words unspoken. How he longed to tell her—to scream—that he loved her, that he had always treasured her, that she had made him the proudest of fathers.

"I failed Cassia most of all. I should have loved her in the way she needed to be loved. I should have tried to understand her more. I should have helped her shoulder the sadness and guilt of losing her mother. Had I been there for her, perhaps none of this would have come to pass. I should have cried with her, lamented with her, and loved with her. Instead, I chose myself above all others. I told myself I was leading a life with Christ, but I was only leading the life I wanted."

Agrippa stepped forward. "You gave us all hope, Decimus. You showed us that joy and peace were possible in this dark and broken world."

Decimus smiled, the lines of regret on his face easing for a brief moment. "Thank you, Agrippa. It grieves me that I won't be the one to officiate your marriage to Dosia. But you deserve a spiritual father more worthy than I. Look for someone who will guide you well."

Dosia took Agrippa's hand in hers.

"Enough of this!" Absalona snapped. "Will you give me your soul willingly or not?"

Decimus's gaze hardened as he turned back to her. "How can I ensure you will keep your end of the bargain?"

Absalona smirked, lifting her hand. With a snap of her fingers, the towering earthen walls surrounding them collapsed. The massive barrier crumbled smoothly back into the ground until only level earth remained.

"You see?" she said. "They are free to leave. Your daughter will also be freed. I have no use for her. She was merely a means to get to you."

The sky darkened abruptly. Ominous clouds rolled in and the air grew hot. Then came the sound—a chilling screech of approaching demons.

They had come. The scavenger demons.

"What are they?" Dosia asked, wide-eyed.

"So, they've come for my soul, too," Decimus said. "I expected them sooner." His tone was calm, almost resigned. To Absalona, he said, "Better make this quick, Absalona, or those demons will take your prize before you can claim it."

"No! Your light is mine!" She bared her fangs at the demons.

Decimus spread his hands wide. "Then come—but remember our deal."

In Cassia's body, Absalona advanced on him. Her lips parted, and she let out a piercing, savage scream. A cloud of red dust spewed forth from her mouth, swirling as it rushed toward Decimus. The dust encircled him, spinning with a dizzying fury.

The storm of red tightened around him. Decimus looked down as his hands and feet began to erode. The disintegration spread rapidly—his arms, his legs, his torso.

His final thought was of Cassia. As his vision dimmed, he caught one last glimpse of her collapsing to the ground, her body finally freed of Absalona's control.

Have mercy, Lord! Have mercy! The prayer echoed in his mind as the red engulfed him completely.

And then there was nothing.

***

Marcia's eyes widened in horror as the last remnants of Decimus vanished into nothingness. In his place stood a figure both mesmerizing and terrifying. Her skin was as pale as moonlight, her long crimson hair flowing like liquid fire. A red robe clung to her lithe form. Her lips were a deep blood red, her eyes a bright red.

Was this Absalona as she had once been?

Above them, the skeletal, flying demons swooped in, their cries echoing, screams of pain and fury.

"We must flee this place before the demons rip us apart!" Agrippa said.

"We can't leave Cassia!" Marcia cried.

She dashed to where Cassia lay, unnoticed by Absalona, whose focus remained on the circling demons.

Marcia dropped to her knees. "Cassia!" She gently slapped her friend's cheeks. "Cassia, please, wake up!"

Cassia's eyes fluttered open, unfocused at first, a dazed look on her face as though waking from a long, heavy sleep.

"Marcia?" she murmured. She blinked, trying to make sense of her surroundings. "Where—?"

"There's no time!" Marcia grasped Cassia's arm, pulling her up to her feet. "I'll explain everything later! For now, we must go!"

The scavenger demons descended, circling like vultures over dying prey. The sickly wind from their wings whipped Marcia's hair around her face as she dragged Cassia forward.

Absalona smiled, her gaze fixed on the descending horde. She bit into her finger, splitting the skin. Dark crimson blood welled up. With a flick of her wrist, she pointed at one of the demons.

From the wound, a thin, needle-like crimson line shot out with blinding speed, striking the demon straight through. The creature screeched before bursting into ashes. The gray remains drifted down like snowflakes, swirling in the dark air.

One by one, Absalona took down the demons. In seconds, the skeletal demons were nothing more than puffs of ash.

When the last demon fell, Absalona lowered her hand and turned her attention to Marcia and the others.

"Now," she said, her voice menacing, "to deal with all of you."

"But what of your promise to Decimus?" Marcia said.

"I promised I would not harm you, and I intend to keep that promise. In fact, I will make you all impervious to pain. I will give you what Decimus so desperately wanted to give you: eternal life."

Vampires. To turn them all into creatures of the night, bound forever to her will.

"I will start with you, dear Marcia."

Absalona stalked toward her.

Beside her, Cassia's fingers tightened around Marcia's hand. Marcia looked to her friend, and in that moment, she saw it.

Cassia was truly back.

But their reunion wouldn't last.

Suddenly, Absalona faltered. She cursed, pressing a hand to her head, her movements jerky and uncoordinated. She struggled, as if some unseen force restrained her, pulling her back from her dark intentions.

Could it be...?

Absalona let out a furious cry and leapt into the air. A brilliant streak of blue light sliced through the space she had just occupied.

Marcia turned toward the source of the light and saw Andreas.

A sigh of relief escaped Marcia's lips, her knees nearly giving out as the tension momentarily lifted.

Finally, the demon slayer had arrived.

X

Absalona landed gracefully, her feet touching down just beyond the deep gouge Andreas's attack had carved into the earth. She straightened, smoothing her crimson robe with a motion that was almost casual, though her eyes never left him.

"You managed to break free of my blood realm," she said. "I cannot say I'm surprised. Though you did it much faster than expected. Well done, demon slayer."

Andreas swiftly scanned his surroundings. Decimus was nowhere to be seen. It seemed he had succeeded in freeing his daughter from Absalona's grip.

But at what cost?

"I think you know the answer to that, my boy."

His heart sank.

"Andreas!" Marcia called out to him.

She stood a short distance away, supporting Cassia, who leaned against her. Marcia's arm wrapped protectively around her friend.

"Marcia," Andreas called back, "are any of you hurt?"

"We are safe. For now."

Andreas nodded, his blade at the ready, though he had extinguished the holy flames for the moment. The glowing embers along its edge dimmed.

"And Cassia—has she returned to herself?"

Cassia lifted her head. Her face was pale, her eyes haunted, but they were her own. She nodded weakly. "I am myself again, but Papa..." Her voice trailed off.

"What happened to the scavenger demons?"

Absalona answered before anyone else could. "Nothing but ash."

Andreas shot Absalona a dark look. While scavenger demons paled in comparison to demon princes, their ferocity in swarms was a force to be reckoned with. Yet she had single-handedly obliterated them all.

"She has absorbed Decimus's light. She is no mere nephil now, my boy."

Andreas hesitated, dread gnawing at him. Summoning the holy flames of his lahat chereb was risky. His previous strike had nearly drained all his aether.

But what choice did he have? This was his duty as a demon slayer.

Andreas called upon the sword's power and blue flames roared across the length of the black blade.

"Have you lost your damned mind?" Andras barked. *"These flames will—"*

Shut it, Andras! I have her!

Andreas clenched his teeth. The holy flames scorched his soul, draining him with every passing second. But he had no time to think of the cost. He had to end this quickly.

"We will have our battle, demon slayer," Absalona said, "but not until I know I can make you mine."

"Running away, then, Absalona?"

She laughed, the sound chilling in its elegance. "You will find me at my sanctuary. I'll be waiting for you there."

She spun and a flurry of crimson swirled around her. In an instant, she was gone. Her demonic presence vanished, and the oppressive weight in the air lifted.

"Damn it..." Andreas growled under his breath.

He dropped to his knees, the blue flames of the sword flickering out.

The others came racing toward him. Marcia reached him first, kneeling by his side and placing a steadying hand on his shoulder.

"Are you hurt, Andreas?"

Andreas forced himself to take deep, calming breaths. "Not hurt," he managed, his voice hoarse. "But my aether...it's near depleted."

"Then it's a blessing Absalona fled when she did," Agrippa said, helping Andreas to his feet.

"You and Dosia are mortal again."

"Thanks to you, Andreas."

The bodies of the Blood Militia lay motionless, rigid in death. There were no signs of struggle.

"What happened here?" he asked.

"We will tell you everything," Dosia said. "But first, we need to treat your wounds, and you need rest."

They retreated indoors, to the house where Andreas had first met Marcia. There, Dosia quickly set about treating Andreas's wounds.

Once his wounds were seen to, they all sat together, sharing a simple meal of bread, olives, and figs. The humble food nourished Andreas, and he could feel his strength returning.

Andreas recounted everything he had encountered at the villa. In turn, Marcia spoke of what had transpired at the village just moments before Absalona had arrived.

"Then Fabian is truly gone?" Dosia asked.

"I'm afraid so. I couldn't save him."

Marcia, seated beside him, placed a comforting hand on his shoulder. "You did everything you could. It's not your fault."

"No, it's mine."

All eyes turned to Cassia. She had been silent since they gathered in the house. She had barely touched her food, her thin frame showing clear signs of malnourishment and exhaustion.

"Cassia—" Marcia started, but Cassia cut her off.

"Well, it's true, isn't it?" She looked at the palms of her hands. "I killed Fabian with my own two hands."

"It was Absalona controlling you," Dosia said. "She is to blame for all of this."

Cassia's hands fell to her sides, her shoulders slumped. Her voice turned hoarse, choked with emotion. "And Papa..."

"He sacrificed himself for you," Marcia said. "For all of us. He loved you, Cassia. He loved you so much he gave his soul over to that demon witch to save you."

"Is there a way to get him back?" Cassia asked Andreas.

Andreas sighed heavily, running a hand through his dark hair. "Valen murdered your father. His spirit lingered in the mortal world, but Absalona consumed him. I can't say with certainty where his spirit is now."

"Perhaps I know," Marcia said, her expression pensive. "Before you arrived, Andreas, Absalona was going to turn us all into her vampires. She was about to pounce on us, and I was certain she would drink our blood—but something stopped her. She looked like she was struggling. Like she warred with herself."

"Ah, interesting," the Deathchaser murmured.

What? Andreas responded internally.

"It appears Absalona has not entirely consumed our dear Decimus. That would explain why she fled instead of crossing swords with you."

But what could be waiting at the temple?

"What else, my boy? Decimus's corpse."

Andreas sprang to his feet. He grabbed his lahat chereb and fastened it securely to his belt. There was no telling what blasphemous act Absalona might commit with Decimus's body.

"Is something wrong?" Marcia asked.

"I have to stop Absalona."

"But your wounds—" Dosia began.

Andreas turned to her, offering a small, reassuring smile. "I'm much better than I was, thanks to you."

"Can you slay her?" Agrippa asked, a sliver of doubt in his tone. It was a fair question. He knew all too well what she was capable of and what was at stake. If Andreas failed, if he fell to her and became her vampire slave, the threat she posed would grow exponentially. Even more lives would be in peril.

"I must."

Cassia shot to her feet. "Let me go with you."

"Absolutely not. The danger—"

"He's my father!" Cassia said, her hands closed into tight fists by her sides. "I need him to know that I love him. I need him to know that he never failed me."

"Cassia, Absalona will use you against me," Andreas said in as calm a tone as he could muster. "I can't protect you and fight her at the same time."

"But—" Cassia began.

"She's much stronger now," Andreas continued. "You must stay here with the others and wait for my return."

"It's for the best, Cassia," Marcia said.

Cassia shook her head. "And if you don't return, what then?"

Andreas studied her for a moment. Despite everything she had endured, she stood strong before him. She had every reason to fall apart, to collapse under the weight of her grief and pain. Yet here she was, willing to face the demon that had cursed her family.

"I like her, my boy. I can see why Absalona possessed her."

Andreas went to her, placing his hands on her shoulders. He looked deeply into her eyes. "Trust me, Cassia. I will avenge your father. I promise you."

Cassia met his gaze, her expression teetering on the edge of heartbreak.

"Be careful," she said.

Andreas gave her shoulders a reassuring squeeze before letting go. And with that, he turned and left them.

ACT FOUR

I

Absalona entered the temple that had once been hers. For generations, many had been sacrificed in her name in this place. This was where her followers had worshiped her, where they had offered her the sweetest of sacrifices—the blood of men and women.

And she had drunk it all. She had had her fill. Until the Romans came and ruined it all.

Her strength had waned after that defeat, her influence reduced to whispers and shadows. But now, after all this time, it was returning. She was becoming what she had once been. And it was all thanks to Decimus.

When Decimus was a boy, she had seen something in him. It stirred her hunger in a way she had not experienced before. She had wanted the boy for herself, to possess him, to feed off of him, to make him hers. When he left with those two damned priests, she thought all was lost and she would never see him again.

But he came back. Of course, he was different—older and experienced. Doubtless, he had traveled far and seen many of the horrors of the Roman Empire. When she saw him, her hunger grew strong again. And this time, she knew what made him special.

His light. He had left her a boy broken and neglected and had come back a man of God. That was what she had seen in him all those years ago.

But was that also what had stopped her back there in the village? She had been moments away from killing Marcia; moments away from draining the pitiful girl's blood.

It had been Decimus. She had heard his voice in her mind telling her no. She had felt him restrain her as though he were physically doing so in the flesh.

She had fed on the blood of countless mortals and not once had any of their blood had this effect on her. She had drunk the blood of heroes and demigods; of giants. They were all like her, a nephil, a creature born from a mortal woman and an angel of the Almighty God.

The same God that had given Decimus his light and that now threatened the control she had.

She now stood over the corpse of the priest. Bending down, she looked over the body. "You belong to me now, Decimus. You hear me? You are mine!"

His light flowed through her. It brought an aetheric power she had not possessed before. With it, she would bring death and suffering to Rome. She was a warrior of renown. She was Absalona, goddess of blood.

And she would not be alone. She would turn all the villagers into vampires, starting with the demon slayer, Andreas.

Doubt wormed its way into her heart. But could she defeat Andreas and make him hers? Or would Decimus interfere?

Footsteps scraped along the dusty floors of her temple. She turned and hissed.

The demon slayer stood at the threshold of the entrance. He slid his black sword from its leather sheath.

"Let us finish this, Absalona."

II

Cassia had been told to rest, but how could she? Her heart raced relentlessly, her mind tangled in turmoil. Absalona's presence still lingered. She could feel it, hear the demon's taunting voice in her thoughts.

It had been two weeks since Valen had killed her father. She hadn't even allowed herself to mourn his passing.

Everything had happened too quickly—vampires, demons, ghosts. The weight of it all was overwhelming. Rest? She doubted she would ever truly rest again. What she sought wasn't rest, but meaning.

With both her parents gone, and the guilt of the monstrous acts she had committed while possessed, she struggled to find a reason to go on. She had blasphemed against her father. She had blasphemed against the Lord.

Her father had taught her the power of repentance: that it was never too late; that every breath was another chance to turn away from the sickness that was sin.

But was it too late for her?

Though Absalona no longer controlled her, the demon had devoured her father's spirit. There was one thing Cassia needed to do: she had to find a way to free her father from the blood goddess.

Cassia stepped out of the room in Marcia's house. Agrippa and Dosia were sitting close together at the wooden table. They had also witnessed, and been part of, Absalona's horrors, yet they seemed calmer now. Perhaps because they were no longer bound by vampirism.

Dosia smiled. "Feeling any better, Cassia?"

"I couldn't sleep."

"That's to be expected," Agrippa said. "Once all this is past us, maybe then you'll find some peace."

She looked away from them. "I'm sorry for what Valen did to you."

"It's not your doing, Cassia," Dosia said, standing up and going to her. "You can't blame yourself."

"If I was stronger... If I had more faith like Papa..."

"We all struggle with our faith," Dosia said. "Your father taught us that. We are just happy that you're safe."

"And you, too." Still, Cassia could not look at them. Shame forced her to look down at her feet. "But Fabian..."

"Is with the Lord in Paradise."

Yes, of course. Fabian was a God-fearing man, humble and gentle. He would find peace in the afterlife. She had no doubt about that.

She looked up at them. "Where is Marcia?"

"She went to the pistrina for more bread."

"I see." Cassia nodded and headed for the door.

"Are you going to go look for her?"

"Yes. I was thinking of going for a walk."

Lord, forgive my lie. Her plan was to catch up with Andreas at the temple.

"I'll go with you," Agrippa said, standing up.

"No, that's all right," she was quick to say. "I'll just find Marcia and we'll walk back together."

"You shouldn't be alone right now."

Cassia nodded. "Thank you, Agrippa. But I'll be fine. Truly."

They reluctantly gave in, and Cassia stepped out of the house, closing the door softly behind her. She took a deep breath, letting the cool air fill her lungs. Pulling her shawl over her head, she hid her face from the villagers. They had seen the horrors Absalona committed through her and there was no telling how they would react if they saw her now, regardless of whether she was still possessed.

Cassia moved through the village, heading for the outskirts. She was almost there when Marcia's voice called out to her.

"You're going to the temple, aren't you?"

Cassia stopped in her tracks, her shoulders stiffening, but she didn't turn to face Marcia. "I have to go. I know it's dangerous. I know Andreas didn't want me to follow him. I know that I am likely to die by Absalona's hand. But if there's a chance that I can see Papa one last time and tell him goodbye, then it's worth it." *Perhaps even save him.* "I am nothing without him."

Marcia drew closer to her.

"Cassia, you have us. We are a church. We are here for you."

"Did you see him? His ghost?"

"I did. But only briefly. His mind was on you. He wanted to make sure you were safe."

Cassia turned to face her, the first person she had made friends with when she and her father decided to settle in this village.

"When Absalona possessed me, I had these...urges. I didn't want to do them. Like with Valen. I had a choice. I could seduce him or not. I always decided not to, but then I would do the exact opposite. It was like it didn't matter what I wanted, as though my will had a mind of its own and I had no control over it. So I did terrible things. I said horrible things." Her voice grew sharper. She reached for Marcia's hand and gripped it tightly. "You have to believe me, Marcia, I didn't want any of it. That's not who I am."

Marcia drew Cassia to her. "I know, Cassia. I know. It was the demon, not you. Agrippa and Dosia described something similar when they were Valen's vampires."

"Valen asked for none of this and was slain for it. The tragedy of it all is too much to bear."

Cassia trembled. Her heart was sick with grieving.

Marcia gave her a small smile, and it was a marvel that she could muster such an expression. "It will all come to an end. Andreas will slay Absalona. He is no ordinary demon slayer. He was known to Decimus and that was why he had me summon for him."

Cassia nodded. "I saw his power when he fought Valen. But it is almost as demonic as Absalona's."

"He, too, has a darkness in him that needs healing. And I pray that one day Christ will heal him."

"Thank you, Marcia. You are all I have left and we aren't even related by blood."

"We are both Christians. You and I are sisters, blood or not. Our bond is in Christ."

"Are you going to stop me from going to the temple?"

Marcia shook her head. "But I have one small request."

"Name it."

"That I come with you."

III

Absalona smiled cruelly, exposing her white fangs. "Have you changed your mind about joining me, Andreas? Are you ready to become my vampire king? I promise you it will only hurt for a moment."

The flames of Andreas's lahat chereb burst over the full length of the blade. "Is this answer enough?"

Absalona tsked. "A pity, but so be it."

She lifted one delicate wrist to her mouth, her sharp fangs sinking into the pale flesh. Then, without hesitation, she repeated the action with her other wrist. Blood did not spill freely as one might expect; instead, it twisted into thin, sinuous tendrils. The crimson strands coiled and swirled around her, filling the air with its metallic scent.

Her eyes flashed crimson, and suddenly shadows spread across the temple floor. They spread quickly, swallowing the space around her until she was entirely enveloped in darkness.

In the blink of an eye, she was gone.

She was using space manipulation and hid in the darkness.

"She has the same powers as Fabian and Valen!"

From the shadows behind Andreas, she released a crimson dart aimed at his throat. He spun around and deflected it with his sword, but more followed—darts hurtling from every direction at blinding speed. Andreas blocked those he could, dodging the rest. His senses strained, trying to locate her demonic presence.

When he finally felt it, he slashed with the lahat chereb through the shadows, but the blow was swallowed up in the darkness.

Absalona's mocking laughter echoed. "I know what you're capable of, demon slayer! You are as good as mine!"

"Now, my boy!"

Andreas tightened his grip on the sword, channeling both its holy power and the dark aether of Andras.

The blue flames shifted to a deep purple, blending with the dark crimson of Andras's demonic energy. The flames roared into an inferno, banishing the shadows and revealing Absalona.

In a flash, Andreas charged at her, lunging forward.

The sword's point pierced through Absalona's shoulder.

He had missed her heart—she had moved just in time.

With a hiss of pain and a seething curse, she leapt back, the blade sliding out of her flesh.

Her blood stained her gown, though it was hardly noticeable as her gown was the color of blood. Crimson blood spilled onto the stone floor, seeping into the cracks and branching out like tiny spiderwebs.

"H-how...?" she managed between heavy breaths.

"When I accepted to host Decimus's spirit within me, it required a great amount of my aether. But now that he no longer inhabits my body, I am able to use my aether to its full potential."

If only for a short time. Already, the aether threatened to overwhelm him. He had enough for one, maybe two, more attacks before his energy was entirely drained.

"You're right. Of course. I was a fool." She stood up, chin raised. "Decimus is not with you anymore. He's mine, both soul and body!"

Andreas frowned. *Soul and...?*

The Deathchaser's voice rang in his mind, *"Behind you!"*

But it was too late—

A hard blow struck Andreas's back, sending him sprawling forward, crashing to the ground. He rolled just in time, narrowly evading another strike.

A splintered piece of a wooden cross smashed into the floor beside him.

The wielder was Decimus's corpse.

IV

Decimus's corpse let out a low growl, flies buzzing around its head while maggots clung to the decaying gray flesh. Its eyes were blank and milky white, and from between its cracked, purplish lips protruded the unmistakable fangs of a vampire.

Absalona had not only reanimated Decimus's corpse but had turned it into one of her own vampires.

Andreas's gaze shifted, noticing the pulsing red tendrils burrowed into the corpse's feet. The blood tendrils led back to their source—the blood goddess herself.

"What I loved about Decimus," Absalona said, "was how subservient he was. First to his parents, even though they despised him, and then to his god, even to the point of ignoring his own daughter. And now to me, even though I will be the end of all he held dear."

With the splintered cross as his weapon, Decimus lunged at Andreas. Andreas rolled to the side, springing back to his feet just in time. Decimus let out a wrathful scream, relentless in his pursuit. He swung the cross again and again, his attacks fierce and unyielding.

Andreas surrendered his sword's flames, sidestepping each blow using only Andras's dark aether.

"What are you doing, my boy? Finish him and be done with it!"

I can't!

Hadn't the priest's body been desecrated enough? Once, this body had been filled with the Holy Spirit. Once, it had been sanctified. And it would one day be resurrected.

"Oh, what's the matter, Andreas? Cannot harm the priest, even if he is my vampire? I assure you his soul is not in that husk. Go on, then—cut him down!"

"She's right, my boy! That is not Decimus! Just an animated corpse!"

I won't do it!

Though the flames of the lahat chereb could reduce the corpse to ashes in moments, Andreas hesitated. He had known Decimus. He had seen the heartbreak in Cassia's eyes when she learned of her father's death. Once this was all over, she would have the chance to give him the burial he deserved.

"Fine, then! Turn your blade to the damned nephil!"

Andreas could do that. His black sword erupted in holy flames once more as he surged toward her.

She stood waiting, arms crossed over her chest, her blood-red lips curling into a taunting smile.

Andreas lunged, thrusting the lahat chereb straight for the nephil's heart—

But he stopped abruptly, the blade's tip hovering over Decimus's chest. Decimus had moved between Andreas and his target, his corpse somehow possessing the speed of a demon. Either that, or Absalona had pulled him into place using the blood tendrils that bound them together.

She ran a hand over the corpse's chin. "If you want me, you'll have to go through him."

"Enough of this! If you won't do it, I will!"

Suddenly, the Deathchaser's dark aether surged, a tingling numbness spreading down Andreas's arms and into his hands.

"No!"

He fought back, resisting with all his strength, refusing to relinquish control of his body to the demon that lurked within.

As Andreas wrested back control, Decimus lunged, wrapping his arms around him in a crushing embrace. Andreas fought desperately, straining to break free from the corpse's iron grip. The overwhelming stench of decay filled his nostrils.

"There's no use struggling," Absalona said. "Decimus has my supernatural speed and strength. And because he is a corpse, he will never tire."

Decimus's grip tightened, and Andreas let out a pained scream, feeling the pressure on his ribs as though they were about to crack. His grasp on the lahat chereb weakened, and the sword fell from his hand, clattering against the temple floor.

Absalona moved slowly around Andreas, her gaze fixed on him as she nudged the black sword away with her foot. "You won't be needing that anymore. A holy sword won't do for my vampire king."

She touched him, tracing her fingers along his shoulders and neck.

"Oh, but you will make for me a fine warrior," she cooed.

Andreas groaned, struggling against the hold, but it was futile.

"Face it, demon slayer—you're mine."

Andreas gasped as Absalona's fangs sank into the nape of his neck.

V

"We're nearly there," Marcia said.

Cassia could see the temple ahead, but something felt wrong. The stone looked painted black, and thick smoke billowed from its openings and main entrance.

A flash of blue light flickered inside, moving like firelight.

Was that Andreas's sword? If so, he was already fighting Absalona.

Then she heard Andreas scream—a cry of pain that made her heart drop. She glanced at Marcia, who met her eyes. Urgency passed between them without a word.

They sprinted the rest of the way.

Reaching the entrance, they peered inside.

There stood Absalona, her fangs sunk deep into Andreas's neck. Andreas's face twisted in agony, his sword lying on the ground, far beyond his reach.

Marcia gasped. "My God. What has she done to him?"

She gestured toward the figure holding Andreas and keeping him locked in place.

But there was no need—Cassia's eyes had already fixed on the animated corpse of her father.

"Papa!" Cassia called out.

Absalona let out a satisfied sigh as she pulled away from Andreas, her mouth stained red, fangs dripping with his blood.

Andreas's strength gave out. His head drooped, his body sagging forward. If not for her father's grip, he would have collapsed to the floor.

"Ah, perfect," Absalona said. "You will be my king's first victims."

With one hand, Absalona lifted Andreas's head, his mouth hanging open. Then she raised one of her bleeding wrists and let it hover over Andreas's lips, allowing her blood to drip into his mouth.

A few drops was all it took.

Decimus's corpse released Andreas and stepped back. But Andreas did not collapse. Instead, he staggered, his hair falling messily over his face.

Then he arched back and let out a guttural howl, his eyes no longer their usual sky blue but a sickly yellow. His gaze locked onto Cassia and Marcia.

Marcia shook her head. "No, Andreas, you must fight this transformation! Please, God!"

Absalona cackled. "Take them, my king!"

Andreas staggered toward them, each step unsteady, as if he were struggling against the pull of his vampiric transformation.

"Papa, what has she done to you?" Cassia cried out, rushing toward her father without a second thought, her only concern to save him.

"Cassia!" Marcia called after her.

Cassia reached Decimus and dropped to her knees, her hands clutching at his decaying robes. She ignored the stench of rot, her eyes seeing past the corpse, trying to remember her father as he once was.

"I know you're still in there, Papa! Please, stop this!" Tears streamed down her face. "Thank you for everything—for giving me life, for protecting me, for making me a daughter of God! Please, come back to us! Lord Jesus Christ, Son of God—"

Her prayer was abruptly silenced as Andreas grabbed her by the throat, lifting her off the ground. His own fangs were visible now. Like Fabian, Dosia, Agrippa, and Valen had been—he was under Absalona's control.

Marcia rushed forward, frantically tugging at Andreas's arms, pleading with him to let Cassia go.

But the demon slayer didn't react, as if Marcia's words were lost to him entirely.

Cassia's father faded from view, her vision blurring as darkness crept in. She gasped, unable to draw breath.

"It's too late, girl," Absalona said standing behind Andreas, watching as the demon slayer squeezed the life out of Cassia. "If you want to be with your father, then become one of my faithful vampi—"

Absalona's eyes widened in shock, and she gave a wet cough. Marcia released Andreas, stepping back with her hands covering her face.

The grip on Cassia's throat loosened, and she gasped as air rushed back into her lungs. She blinked away tears, her vision clearing enough to see what Marcia was seeing.

The blade of Andreas's sword protruded from Absalona's chest, thrust straight through her heart.

"W-what...?" Absalona stammered, blood bubbling from her lips. "Decimus...you..."

Her father's corpse spoke, his voice raspy and strained. "Leave...my...family...alone..."

He yanked the sword free, and Absalona dropped to her knees, her blood pouring down the length of her gown. She turned to face Decimus, blood-tinged tears streaking her pale face.

"But Decimus...I...love...you..."

Decimus gripped the sword with both hands and swung it across her neck, severing her head cleanly from her body.

VI

Andreas blinked, his senses returning only to reveal his hand wrapped around Cassia's throat. Trembling, he slowly released his grip, pulling his hand away.

"What am I doing?" he said.

Marcia clung to his arm, her eyes wet with tears. "Have you returned to us?"

"Marcia?"

"My boy, you were a vampire and under Absalona's control. She drank your blood and forced you to drink hers."

Yes, now Andreas remembered. He touched his neck, feeling the two raised lumps where Absalona's fangs had punctured his skin. He recalled the darkness:

thick and endless, like being submerged in an icy void. He could feel neither Andras nor any real sense of himself.

He had been lost, consumed by vampirism.

But now he was back, mortal once more, the vampirism undone. If that was true, it could only mean one thing.

Absalona was dead.

"But how?" he whispered to himself.

"It was not my doing. The vampirism blocked even my reach."

"Papa, it's you."

Andreas followed Cassia's gaze, turning to look behind him. There lay Decimus's corpse, lifeless and still as death. But Cassia's eyes weren't on the body.

They were on the ghostly form of her father.

"Yes, I am here," Decimus said, a warm smile spreading across his face as he looked at his daughter. "I heard your words. They pierced through Absalona's darkness. They gave me courage to finally break free of her."

"Papa, I'm so sorry. This is all my fault."

Decimus shook his head. "No, my Cassia. The fault is all mine. I should have been a better father to you. I was blind to my own pride. I thought if I sought only

God I would be blessed. But little did I know that loving God meant loving others as well. And what is love but sacrifice? I should have devoted myself to you and the others. Please forgive me for hurting you."

"I do. I always will."

Decimus turned to Marcia. "Marcia, will you take care of my daughter? Will you accept her into your family?"

Marcia came to stand beside her friend and took Cassia's hand in hers. "Of course, Father. She is my sister."

"Thank you. And you, Andreas. Thank you for all that you've done."

Andreas nodded, taking note of both the blood on his sword and the headless body of Absalona.

Decimus's countenance darkened. "I don't have much time left."

"What do you mean?" Cassia asked. "Can't you stay?"

"I wish I could, daughter. But they've come for me."

A shrill screech tore through the air as scavenger demons burst through the temple's roof, chunks of stone falling as they clawed their way in. Andreas quickly counted over ten of the frail-looking but dangerous demons.

He went and picked up his lahat chereb. One good thing about becoming a vampire was that it had rejuvenated his aether and completely healed his wounds.

He summoned the holy flames.

But Decimus stayed his hand. "No, Andreas. Let them be."

"His soul is ours," a scavenger said. "Would you deny us, slayer of our kind?"

Even if Andreas did slay them all, more would come. He could not fend against them all.

"Is this what you truly want?" Andreas asked.

"I cannot run forever," Decimus answered. "Even as a ghost."

Andreas extinguished the flames and sheathed his sword. "Very well. May God have mercy on you."

Decimus nodded. "May He have mercy on us all." He turned to his daughter one final time. "I love you, Cassia. Always remember that."

And then the demons took him.

Epilogue

Marcia returned to the village and brought both Dosia and Agrippa to the temple. Together, they dug a grave for Decimus by a tree just outside the ruined temple. Agrippa found a cross inside that was relatively in one piece and planted it at the head of the grave. Andreas led them through a short prayer for the dead, one he had learned from the monks at Mount Athos.

"Andreas," Marcia asked, "what will become of Decimus now that the demons have taken his soul?"

"It is difficult for me to say. It's believed that those who have done truly horrible sins from which they did not repent in their lifetime may experience a foretaste of the Lake of Fire in the very depths of Hades before the Day of the Lord."

"The demons said that his soul was there," Cassia said. She had been strong throughout the burial and prayer, and there was a quiet acceptance about her. Though both her parents were gone from the mortal world, she still had family that cared deeply for her, a brother and two sisters in Christ. "Is there nothing we can do for Papa?"

"There is always hope, for our God is a God of hope and mercy."

"Then what must we do for our spiritual father?" Agrippa asked.

"Pray for him," Andreas said. "Pray for God's mercy. We must all pray for those who have departed."

"Will the Lord hear our prayers?" Cassia asked.

Andreas nodded. "He always does. Pray with all your heart, soul, and mind, and perhaps one day your father will break free from the shackles of Hades."

"Is that truly possible?"

"It is."

Intercessory prayer of this kind was the greatest gift one could give to a departed loved one, for there was no way for that loved one to return such kindness. Andreas had no doubt that Decimus would one day see the Paradise that the Lord had in store for his beloved children.

Andreas promised them that he would have Mount Athos send a new spiritual father to them, and they made plans to give Fabian a proper burial.

With the mission completed, Andreas said his farewells and headed on his way back to Iader. He would need rest before he and his black sword were called again.

"I wonder, my boy, who will pray for you when your time comes?"

"You've been quiet for some time," Andreas said to his demon.

"Oh, just reminiscing about our dear Decimus."

"You miss him, don't you?"

"Heaven forbid! Though as far as priests go, I suppose he wasn't all that infuriating. After all, he did commit a weighty sin. I must give him credit for that."

Andreas couldn't help but smile.

"I only hope my fellow demons show him a modicum of mercy."

Andreas heard low-pitched soothing notes. Birdsong.

The calming sound came from a white dove perched on a hanging tree branch. It seemed to look at Andreas before it spread its wings and soared high into the skies.

Yes—Andreas was certain Decimus would see Paradise.

MASTER'S
APPRENTICES
DEMON
SLAYER
ROME
PREQUEL
GEORGE
ALEXANDROS

About the Author

George Alexandros is the Greek-Canadian author of the Demon Slayer Rome series and the indie game developer of the turn-based RPG series, Elohim Eternal.

https://georgealexandros.net

george@georgealexandros.net

Also by the Author

Novels

DEMON SLAYER ROME

Master's Apprentices

Beneath the Mire

Ghost of Perdition

Video Games (available on Steam)

ELOHIM ETERNAL

Elohim Eternal: The Babel Code

Elohim Eternal: Exodus

Elohim Eternal II: Son of Man

www.ingramcontent.com/pod-product-compliance
Lightning Source LLC
LaVergne TN
LVHW091654230426
836993LV00002B/50
* 9 7 8 1 9 8 8 8 3 8 1 0 6 *